PINK SAND SUMMER

PINK SAND SUMMER

Chassity Evans

CONTENTS

This is for the girls.

Our first loves, our constants,
the ones we return to again and again.
Forever among the greatest loves of our lives.

Chapter One

THE GUY SITTING ACROSS FROM ME LOOKS EXACTLY LIKE THE kind of guy I'd flirt with on vacation. But this isn't exactly a vacation. I'm flying into the remains of someone else's life and pretending I know what to do with it.

He's got a canvas notebook open, pen racing like he's trying to catch a thought before it escapes as wavy, sandy brown hair falls carelessly over his eyes. His T-shirt is perfectly worn, and he's got earbuds in like he's tuning out the world. He hasn't looked up once. I've risked two quick glances in this five-minute boat ride.

Around us, the water glimmers, all impossible blues. As we cut through the shallow channel between Eleuthera and Harbour Island, I lean into the breeze. This is the part I always forget I need. The separation. The five minutes of nothing but sea and salt to clear everything out. If I can just get through this summer without falling apart, maybe I'll believe this place can belong to me.

I glance down at the manila folder inside my tote. "Bahamas Docs" is scrawled across the front in Mr. Hasell's lawyerly script, like it's a grocery list instead of a life handed over. Straight ahead, Harbour Island is beckoning like a lifelong best friend. It's always felt like mine in the ways that matter. And now, the house is mine, too, but it still feels like I'm borrowing something too sacred to claim. Gran left me Lazy Daisy like it was obvious, like it wasn't the biggest thing anyone's ever handed me. Nothing like inheriting a house to remind me I'm still the kind of person who can't keep a fiddle leaf fig alive. But maybe it does make sense. Summer after summer, no matter what, I'm most alive here.

Across from me, Notebook Guy shifts, stretching one leg out into the space between us. He pauses his scribbling long enough to glance up through his wind-tousled hair, and when our eyes catch, he gives me a slow, subtle smile. I return it quickly, running my hand through my hair, conscious that I've been awake since five a.m.

When we dock, a deckhand wearing a Bahamas Life T-shirt hands me my suitcase as I step onto the pier.

"Lucy!"

Mr. Franklin's voice rolls down the dock like a welcome mat. One of a handful of taxi drivers on the island, Mr. Franklin's golf cart is as much a landmark as the "Welcome to Harbour Island, Home of Friendly People" sign. He's leaning against it, one foot propped on the bumper like he has nowhere else to be. Same salt-and-pepper beard, same motor oil scent when he hugs me.

"You're your grandmother's girl," he says, giving me a once over. "You look just like her standing here."

My throat tightens, but I smile. "Thanks for picking me up, Mr. Franklin."

"Wouldn't let anyone else do it," he says, already tossing my suitcases on the back. Just before we pull away, I catch Notebook Guy, still by the dock, eyes lingering on me.

We drive through town, past pastel-painted shops and familiar porches. Everyone waves, nodding "g'day, g'day" like no time has passed. Yet for me, everything feels different, untethered. As the golf cart climbs the hill, I press my palms against my knees, bracing myself.

We pass the guest cottage where Milly lives, the shutters freshly painted their soft green. She's been here at Lazy Daisy since I was a little girl, slipping me benne cakes when Gran said I'd had enough sugar, braiding my hair on the porch when I begged. Calling her a house manager doesn't do justice to what she means to me.

And then the main house rises into view. Lazy Daisy, steady as always, but somehow changed. The bougainvillea has gone wild since last summer, spilling from the fence line and climbing the porch columns. Once young and tentative, now it's in riotous bloom, bold, bright, unapologetically alive. The chaotic color daring me to stop pretending I've got everything under control.

Mr. Franklin whistles low. "She's still the prettiest one on the block if you ask me."

I nod and smile, grateful for my sunglasses hiding my glistening eyes. Seeing the house in person again, the weight of responsibility settles differently than it did in the lawyer's office.

Mr. Franklin drops my bags on the porch, shaking me out of my daydream. "Margaret kept this house full of life. Probably a few stories in these walls, I'd bet."

I nod, my hand already on the worn brass doorknob. "I'd bet that, too. Thanks, Mr. Franklin."

He gives me a wink and disappears down the path. I smile, sliding off my sunglasses as I turn to face the light blue front door. If I can just get through this first night alone in the house without calling my friend Dawn to come rescue me, maybe I'll actually make it through the summer. I turn the handle and push the door open. The house smells like lemon oil and old paper. The floors gleam, the cushions are fluffed, and there's a note from Milly on the entry table in her looping handwriting: *"Welcome home. Call if you need anything."*

I pause, letting the quiet settle around me. That kind of quiet that only comes from a place that's been lived in and loved well. I walk into the living room, across the jute rug and worn floorboards, and finally exhale.

Upstairs, I pass two guest rooms with their windows open to catch the sea breeze. One has a shell collection on the nightstand. The second still holds the dog-eared copy of *Pride and Prejudice* Gran claimed was "for ambiance" but reread every September. The natural light in this room would lend itself well to a home art studio. Maybe by the end of summer, I'll have something worth showing on a gallery wall again…or at least a sketch that doesn't end up in the trash.

My room is at the end of the hall. The door creaks just like always, and the wallpaper wraps me in a hug, that faded floral grass cloth in blush and sage, comforting in a way that makes my throat ache. The bed is made in crisp white linens, a pale green throw folded at the foot. I drop my suitcase and sit down slowly, running my hand across the quilt. Everything is the same. And somehow, not. I unpack. I always do it first thing. Soft tees, shorts, pajamas, and swimsuits into the dresser drawers. Dresses and gauzy coverups in the closet.

I slip on my black string bikini. The bathroom tile is cool under my feet, white hex with little green insets that form a loose star pattern. The glass jar of cotton balls is full. The monogrammed hand towels look perfectly pressed.

Downstairs, I grab an oversized beach towel from the basket near the back door and step out onto the porch. The ocean rolls ahead of me, that low steady pull I've never been able to resist. I cross the lawn, bougainvillea brushing my shoulder as I pass through the arbor gate.

It's quiet on the beach, and the light pink sand is warm and soft under my feet. Harbour Island is known for its pink sand beaches. The saturation can vary, but the hue is always a light pink. And the water is an impossibly clear turquoise. It's my favorite color combo in the world. I walk straight in until I'm deep enough to float on my back.

"Lucy."

I shoot up in the water, the thud of my heart proving that my body recognized him before my brain could. I'd know his voice anywhere.

Jack, with his all-consuming presence. He removes his sunglasses, revealing rich, hazel eyes, sharp jawline, and a dimple that I've always loved. His shirt clings to his shoulders, irritatingly broader than the last time I saw him. His wavy hair, usually kept under control, has gotten a little unruly in a way that makes him even more appealing.

His grin flashes, quick and unguarded, gone almost before I catch it, as if he's yanked the curtain closed on something too revealing. The water foams around his feet, but it's the flicker in his eyes, mirroring my own disbelief, that holds me rooted in place. Jack, who is so familiar and yet feels like a stranger.

I'm still closing the last step between us when his arms pull me in. It's instinctual, our years of practice to thank for that. Muscle memory is rude. His shirt comes away wet, but he doesn't seem to care. We both take an awkward step back, his eyes squinting from the sun as he searches my face.

"I didn't know you were here."

"I wasn't," I say, barely able to meet his focused gaze. "I mean, I just got here."

His expression softens, "I'm so sorry about your grandmother. The island feels different without her."

"It does." My voice drops. "Thank you for being at the funeral. I'm sorry we didn't get a chance to talk."

"It's okay, Lucy," he says gently. He doesn't press, and the quiet expands until I can't stand it.

"She left me the house." I still haven't figured out the correct tone for that sentence.

His eyebrows jump, then ease as something warmer takes hold of his expression. "Wow. That's…big."

I nod. "I'm still figuring it out."

"She always said you belonged here."

I nod, twisting a ring on my finger. Jack glances up toward the house, then back to me.

"How have you been? It's been too long." His eyes squint, almost as if it hurts to acknowledge it. "I heard you have a new gallery?"

"Yeah, it's a shared studio space and gallery with a few artist friends where we…share space…for art." Yikes.

Jack's eyes soften as a smile tugs at the corners of his annoyingly full lips. "A shared studio where you share space?"

I look down and smile through a blush. Fantastic.

"I'd like to see what you've been working on."

"Honestly, you haven't missed much. I've been staring at a blank canvas for weeks."

Something flickers in his eyes, maybe a reminder of the gap between our then and our now. He checks his watch, grimacing. "I'm supposed to be on a call in ten minutes. What about later? Can you come over for a margarita?"

His voice is relaxed, but his eyes flick over my face, eager in a way that betrays the laidback tone. Before I can overthink it, I reply, "Sure, I'll see you later." So much for spending my first night alone.

He backs away with a crooked smile. "You look really good, Luce."

I tell myself that means nothing. Obviously. And I keep my smile easy as I watch him disappear up the steps of the house two doors down from mine. The slam of his gate lingers in the quiet of the waves, so I fall backward into the surf, willing the saltwater to carry off my thoughts. It doesn't.

Back inside, I peel off my swimsuit and hang it on the orange-striped ceramic fishhook on the bathroom door, placed dead center so I could reach it as a child.

Downstairs, I drift through the family room. Everything looks the same, but it doesn't feel that way. Rattan chairs slouched with cushions in faded florals and stripes. The vintage game table in the corner, Mahjong tiles stacked neatly, as if someone might sit down any minute. I drag my fingers over the cool green pieces, listening to their faint clink.

Sunlight washes the pecky cypress walls to honey. The lamp brought back from our Paris trip. The framed island map with Gran's penciled notes curling into the margins. A bowl of conch shells exactly where it's always been. I take it in quickly, like proof that this is all really mine.

In the kitchen I pour a glass of water into one of the heavy green glasses and curl into the window seat, knees pulled to my chest. The cushions give under my weight as I stare out at the glimmering ocean.

The look in Jack's eyes keeps replaying, low and steady, and the echo of his voice, *you look really good, Luce*, makes my heart race despite my better judgement. I can't let those words and that look mean anything. Because even though I'd never admit it out loud, I don't trust myself to choose love without handing my heart over only to be hurt again.

This house, this island…it holds every version of me. The good ones. And the messy ones. The girl who thought love could last forever if you just believed hard enough. The girl who found out it could vanish faster than a summer storm.

Maybe Gran had her versions, too. I think about the jewelry box I found last summer, tucked inside her dresser. Not jewelry inside, but an old photograph of her with a man I didn't recognize, though the camera only captured his profile. Not Granddad. Her only explanation: "The best lives have lots of chapters, sweetheart. Doesn't mean they're meant to be the ending."

Chapter Two

MY STOMACH GROWLS LOUD ENOUGH TO ECHO, AND I REALIZE I haven't eaten since that airport latte and the granola bar on the flight. It's the kind of hunger that sneaks up on you when you're distracted. I open the kitchen drawer and curl my fingers around the keys to Gran's Jolly. The frayed pink-and-green friendship bracelet is still looped through the ring, the one I made when I was nine and insisted she keep forever. She did. Of course she did. By the door, a rack of straw totes hangs on the wall. Island made. I snag one as I head outside. Everything in this house has a purpose, even the decor.

Across the lawn, the garage door creaks open, revealing the light blue Fiat Jolly with its open-air sides, caramel wicker seats, and blue-and-white striped canopy. It looks like a beach postcard come to life. Gran adored it. It was the last gift Gramp ever gave her.

I slide behind the wheel, the wicker already warm in this heat, and coax the engine to life. It coughs, then settles, stubborn as ever. The shade of blue matches Lazy Daisy's shutters.

As I roll past her cottage, I spot Milly on her porch. She's in black linen pants and a fitted short sleeve gray tee, always efficient but still pulled together. Her cropped black hair glints in the sun as she looks up, already clocking me. Nothing on this island happens without Milly noticing.

"Well, would you look who's back," she sings, rising to meet me as I hop out for a hug.

"It's so good to see you," I say, wrapping my arms around her. Milly has always been part-aunt, part-big sister, part-savior.

She pulls back and wipes her eyes. "Margaret sure is missed around here, Lucy."

We stand there for a moment, letting it hang in the air.

Then I remember. "I was hoping we could go over some of the house stuff sometime this week."

"How's nine tomorrow morning?"

"Perfect," I smile, and she squeezes my hand before stepping back.

Five minutes later I'm parked in front of the Piggly Wiggly. Our grocery store is small and always requires a bit of improvisation. I grab the basics, plus cheese, crackers, fruit, and water, because island logic says you should always have snacks on hand.

From there, I swing by Tip Top, our general store that sells everything from pillow inserts to starfruit. The owner is restocking the produce basket with pineapples from her farm on Eleuthera, the larger main island next door. I pick the best one and add more cheese from the little fridge in the back.

I load the bags into the passenger seat of the Jolly and head back toward the house, mentally calculating how much time

I have to shower and get ready before margaritas at Jack's. The answer is enough, *if* I don't overthink it.

I'm passing the island's little pink library when a golf cart flies around the bend, way too centered in the lane.

I swerve, heart in my throat. The cart jerks back just in time, and we miss each other by inches. Cool. Great. Love a casual brush with death before dinner.

As we pass, I lock eyes with the driver, annoyed. He looks terrified, hands tight on the wheel.

Oh. It's him. Notebook Guy. My pulse spikes for an entirely different reason now, which feels unfair given the circumstances. He glances over his shoulder as he slows to a stop and offers me a sheepish wave.

"Sorry about that," he calls. "I'm not used to driving on the wrong side of the road."

I've pulled to the shoulder, half-turned in my seat to face him. His golf cart idles several yards away.

"You don't say," I call back, my heart still trying to catch up.

He gives a charming, lopsided grin. "I'll do better?"

I can't tell if it's the heat or the near miss making my face warm. Or that grin. A cart pulls up behind him, so he waves again, then shifts into drive and disappears around the curve.

This island is full of surprises today.

After I finish putting the groceries away, I head back upstairs to shower. The sun's dropping lower now, casting a golden glow across the yard and straight into my bedroom windows.

I try on a few things before settling on a short, creamy white linen dress. It's fitted at the waist, skimming just enough over my hips to feel quietly dangerous. The neckline twists at one shoulder, leaving the other bare.

I study my reflection, tilting my head. It's definitely too much. Which makes it perfect.

I leave it on. Jack and I have a long history of breaking each other's hearts, a pattern that has repeated too often. And every summer, that inexplicable pull returns. Honestly, who am I kidding? That pull lasts all year long.

I twist my hair into a loose knot, a few blonde strands slipping free to graze my shoulders. It's the kind of golden that always lightens after a few days here, like even my hair knows where it is. I glance at myself once more. Sun-kissed, a little flushed, blue-green eyes brighter than usual thanks to salt air and a day spent outside.

Fine. This is happening.

Downstairs, I queue up something upbeat and lay out wedges of cheese and glossy fruit, arranging them over a platter. I don't overthink it. I grab the house keys and head out, the evening air thick with charcoal smoke from a neighbor's grill and the promise of margaritas I should probably be nervous about. Probably.

The path between our houses is worn into me as much as the sand, every step a muscle memory of summers past, bare feet, quick dashes, stolen moments.

I've been in love with Jack since I was sixteen. Back then, I was just Allie's friend, always tagging along, pretending I didn't notice the way he'd run his hands through his hair or tease me like I was still a kid. It took several more summers before he started seeing me differently, and by then it was already too late. I was gone for good.

That's the thing about us. Every summer we find our way back to each other, like the tide doesn't know any better. But once we return to our real lives, his in New York, mine in

Charleston, it eventually all falls apart. But he spent last summer in London. Which means other than the twelve seconds in the receiving line at Gran's funeral, this is the first time I've seen him in nearly two years.

I climb Jack's porch like I've done a hundred times before, the boards creaking under my feet. Pausing, platter in hand, I remind myself what I've been rehearsing all day: I will not fall for Jack this summer.

"There you are." His grin is just a little too eager as he opens the door.

"Guess I still know my way," I say, slipping past, my shoulder faintly catching his.

The kitchen smells like grilled sausage and lime, and there's music playing somewhere in the background, something old and easy. Jack takes the platter from me and sets it on the counter next to a half-sliced lime and a bottle of tequila.

"I had to make do with island groceries," I grin, stabbing a cube of cheese with a toothpick and popping it in my mouth.

He reaches for the shaker, wrist flexing as he tips it. When he slides the glass toward me, rim half salted, just the way I like it, my eyes snag on his hands. I've felt those hands touch me hundreds of times, yet somehow they look different now. Stronger, rougher, like the city hasn't managed to sand down the boy who spent summers fixing boats and hauling gear for his dad.

He leans back against the counter, sipping. His brown eyes are steady on mine as I catalog the pale green button-down, sleeves rolled, collar open—definitely new. Maybe a girlfriend picked it out. Maybe a current girlfriend. The thought stings, and I take a bigger sip than I mean to.

"So," I say, setting my glass down firmly, "how's the family? I can't wait for Allie to get here."

Allie is Jack's younger sister. She's my age and has remained one of my closest friends since childhood. And not just because she was two doors down. Allie is a genuinely good human. The kind that I could always trust with my deepest secrets. She and her husband Drew just had a baby, the first baby in our friend group, and I'm dying to get my hands on him.

"Yeah, me too. I'll move out to the guest cottage when they get here so they can have the house to spread out a little."

"You'll definitely sleep better out there," I laugh, the sound a little lighter than I feel.

I slip onto a barstool, my woven sandals dropping with a soft thud. His gaze flicks down quickly, and I cross my legs slowly, heat rising as I feel his eyes tracing over me.

"So, you said you're not painting much these days?"

I shrug, twisting the stem of my glass in frustration. "Trying. I guess I've felt uninspired the last couple of months. I managed to finish all my commissions, but what I really need is to start on a new collection."

Something familiar flickers across his face, the way he used to look when he wanted to fix something. Before either of us can say more, footsteps thud on the porch. Dawn's voice carries in ahead of her.

"Oh." I wince, setting my glass down. "I forgot to tell you. I invited Dawn."

Jack's smile comes a little too quick. "That's great. I've barely seen her."

The front door swings wide. "All right," Dawn calls, vowels clipped just so, unmistakably posh. "Where are you hiding her?"

People always assume she's from London, but Dawn's as Harbour Island as pink sand, just shaped by a childhood spent shuttling between home and very proper English boarding schools.

"In the kitchen," I shout back, and a second later she's sweeping in, all long limbs and confidence, her braids pulled back and her dark skin glowing against a yellow dress that hugs her frame like it was made for her.

She throws her arms around me in a twirling embrace, and then she turns to Jack with a glare.

"You avoiding me, Jack?"

"Caught," he lifts his hands in surrender. "Work's been busy."

"Then you're overdue," Dawn says, taking the margarita he offers, tipping her chin at him in that old, familiar way. Her gaze slides back to me, already scheming. "Gusty's later?"

"I could be swayed," I grin.

Dawn is already halfway through Jack's cabinets, hunting for chips the way she's done since middle school. Our banter falls into familiar grooves, Dawn teasing Jack about squeezing limes like he's auditioning for a commercial. Jack firing back about her epic teenage crush on the Gusty's bartender and how she'd ask him for extra lime slices just for an excuse to talk to him. And me rolling my eyes and laughing at them both. Jack leans a little closer whenever I speak, the way he always did, and I don't miss the way Dawn clocks it, her brows twitching.

Just before ten, we climb into Jack's golf cart, the wind dismantling my hair as we roll toward the north end of the island. Gusty's is perched on the hill above the bay. It's beloved for its sand dance floor and the shots served in a shot ski. Jack parks with one hand stretched on the back of my seat just like he used to. He probably doesn't mean anything by it, but I notice.

We're greeted by locals, seasonal regulars, and tourists who look like they've just claimed their new favorite bar. Dawn disappears to say hello to someone by the bar, while Jack leads me to a table on the patio that catches the breeze off the water. He sets a Sands beer in front of me and raises his own in a salute.

"To summer," he says.

I smile and tap my bottle against his. "Summer never disappoints."

The words leave my mouth and there's a brief pause, so quick anyone else would miss it. Jack takes a sip of his beer, gaze drifting toward the water before returning to me.

Summer is easy for us. It always has been. Fall is where things get complicated. I remember one October afternoon, me calling from my old studio in Charleston, paint still drying on my hands, him answering from a yellow cab in New York, horns blaring behind him. I was trying to tell him about a new piece, and he was checking the time before another meeting. That was always how it went. Here on Harbour Island, we find each other. Out there, we lose each other.

I glance over my shoulder as I take a sip, and there he is. Notebook Guy.

He's standing near the pool table, talking to someone but not really watching them. His eyes are on me. And he doesn't look away. My pulse jumps, and I look down, pretending to smooth my dress. When I glance back, he's still watching.

Dawn slides back into her seat. "One of the resort owners just confirmed what I've been saying. This is going to be Harbour Island's busiest summer ever."

Jack leans back. "Should be good for sales at your shop, then."

Dawn nods with a grin, then turns to me. "You're around all season, right Luce?"

"Yeah," I say, brushing a piece of hair from my face. "Through August. I had my painting supplies shipped ahead. I'm hoping they'll show up on the boat next week."

"What are you working on?" Dawn asks.

I shake my head. "Nothing. Yet. But I'm thinking about starting on an island-inspired collection…I'm not sure."

Dawn tilts her head. "Something wild and beachy. You haven't done that in a long time."

"Maybe," I reply, glancing over at the group of girls dancing on the sand.

Jack shifts his beer bottle from one hand to the other. "I'll be here most of the summer, too. Maybe a couple quick trips back for work if I have to."

"God, please tell me you're not going to ghost us again like last year," Dawn says, leveling a finger at him.

"I was working in London," he protests.

Dawn narrows her eyes.

"I'm here now," he insists earnestly, looking over at me.

Dawn lets it slide, steering the conversation to a story about a jewelry shipment gone wrong at her boutique. I nod along, but I'm immediately frustrated by his London comment. Of course he missed being in his favorite place because of work.

My fingers fuss with the label on my beer. Restless. Distracted. And almost every time I glance toward Notebook Guy, five times now (who's counting), I catch him glancing back, jolts of eye contact, each one a little sharper than the last. He doesn't stare, doesn't leer. Just watches, like he's curious. Maybe a little amused.

Jack waves a hand in front of me. "Earth to Lucy."

I blink hard, heat rising to my cheeks. "Sorry. Think the day's catching up to me." I push my chair back, suddenly needing distance. "I'm gonna grab some water."

At the bar, I order three bottles, palms pressed flat against the counter like it'll ground me. By the time I return to our table, I've mostly pulled myself together. Notebook Guy and his friends are finishing up, laughter tapering as they stack their cues. My pulse ticks faster with every step they take toward the door. I brace for something, a word, a nod, anything. But he doesn't stop. The air shifts as he passes, and just before he's gone, his eyes find mine with one last look and a subtle nod.

Chapter Three

THE HOUSE IS QUIET AS I MOVE THROUGH THE KITCHEN AND start mixing up a box of blueberry muffins, timing them to be fresh out of the oven at nine. Milly's always punctual. And she has a sweet tooth. Never mind that I could eat five myself right now.

Morning light pours through the windows in wide slants, covering the counter and the manila folder with patterned light. I slide it closer, my fingers catching the edge, and suddenly I'm back in that office in Charleston.

"She wanted you to have the house, Lucy. She was clear about that," Mr. Hassell says.

I nodded, but it didn't quite hit me. I signed the papers and walked out like my life hadn't just changed shape. Now, standing here slightly hungover in her kitchen, I open the folder again. Inside, it's all still there, deed papers, account info, a note Gran wrote in her shaky but unmistakable hand.

"Take care of this place, and it will take care of you. The walls hold more than memories. They'll always remind you who you are."

Behind the note is a typed letter from Mr. Hasell, outlining the basics of a trust that Gran set up. Enough to cover upkeep, taxes, some repairs if I'm careful. I press my thumb against the curve of her signature.

Right on time, I hear Milly's voice from the front porch. "Yoohoo, Lucy!"

"Come on in, Milly," I call out.

She steps into the kitchen carrying a spiral notebook with a plate of cookies stacked on top.

I smile. "Are those chocolate chip?"

"Wouldn't dream of bringing anything else," she laughs, setting them down on the island. "It's fixing to be a beautiful day, so let's get this boring stuff over quickly, shall we?"

She plants her hands on her hips and grins. "I can see that look. You're already ten steps ahead in your mind. But trust me, this part's simple. We'll be through it in no time."

We settle in at the breakfast table with the blueberry muffins between us. Milly opens the notebook and dives in, running through everything. She's already compiled a list of contacts, service providers, and account details, bless her. She'll continue managing the day-to-day maintenance of the house, and I can handle any payments from the RBC account here in the Bahamas. I need to go by the bank to get that all settled.

"I'd been telling Margaret over the last year that we'd need to look at replacing the garage roof soon," Milly says, flipping a page.

"I just noticed it yesterday," I nod. "I should probably handle it before hurricane season, don't you think?"

"I'll have Jay come take a look," she says, jotting it down in her notes.

"You're a lifesaver, Milly. I don't know how I'd do this without you." Especially from Charleston. It feels almost manageable with her here to help.

"I've been thinking about something. I know Gran never wanted to rent out the house…but I'm considering it. What do you think?"

Milly leans forward, eyes bright. "I think it's a wonderful idea. It'd be a shame for this pretty house to sit empty too much. You could ease into it, start by renting to friends of friends."

"That's a good idea."

She scans the room. "We'll need to declutter a little, too. Just a little freshening up."

I nod, already thinking about the closets in Gran's room. After we finish, Milly leaves me with the notebook she prepared, neatly tabbed and more organized than anything I could've pulled together. I can almost picture it, guests coming and going, the house pulsing with life again. My shoulders relax as I tuck the notebook under my arm, a small spark of possibility flickering.

I pull my hair up and decide it's time. If I'm going to rent this place someday, I need to start cleaning and organizing, especially Gran's suite.

I begin in her bedroom. The chaise where she used to read with the stack of *Town & Country* magazines fanned out. The closet doors creak slightly when I open them. Inside, the walk-in is like stepping into a time capsule of quiet elegance. Her rose perfume lingers on the racks of dresses in every shade of white, cream, and blush. Her signature wide brim hats hang on pegs beside a single straw bag with slightly frayed handles.

I start slowly, pulling out pieces one by one and putting them into piles. Keep. Donate. Maybe. I'll call Mom later to see what she and Dad might want. I fold carefully, setting aside a few pieces I know I'll never part with. I find one of Gran's old caftans folded carefully at the back of a shelf, pale coral silk with a delicate neckline of beading. I hold it up and smile. The memories are so vivid they feel alive. Of friends, a mix of locals and part-timers, our bonds deepened season after season. We'd fill our days on the beach, running up to Tip Top for candy and snacks, and sneaking over to Grandfather's Beach.

As we got older, we'd take boats out to quieter beaches on nearby islands, where a lot more exploring, and a lot more firsts, happened. The freedom we had here was a teenage dream. Loose curfews. Late-night dock parties. Tan lines we'd spent hours working on, and laughter echoing into the dark.

While we were off adventuring, the adults would spend lunch hours at Coral Sands' deck, overlooking the beach. It has one of the best views on the island. Dinners rotated between houses. There was always something, a cocktail hour, a garden party, a beach bonfire. And we were never excluded from the festivities. That was the magic of it. We were expected to show up. Dressed. On time. Ready to mingle.

By the age of sixteen my friends and I were sneaking Rum Dums and Goombay Smashes, carrying on lively conversations at the dinner table with far too much confidence. Gran said one should never underestimate the importance of social skills. As a result, I've always been able to hold my own at any dinner table with any guest. I don't think Gran knew about the Rum Dums, but then again, nothing got past her.

The parties were always chic but unfussy. You'd spot celebrities, swimsuit models from whatever magazine or catalogue shoot was happening on the beach, sometimes even royals. At one dinner, I was seated next to an actual princess. I was surprised by how normal she was. We hit it off and still spend time together whenever she visits.

Nothing was too perfect. The power would cut out. Storms would roll in out of nowhere. We'd end up dressing in the dark, eating and dancing by candlelight. It only made the moment better.

I press the caftan to my chest, then fold it gently and place it in the "keep" pile.

Chapter Four

I WAKE UP EARLY THE NEXT MORNING TO THE CROW OF ROOST-ers, Harbour Island's natural alarm clock, with that pleasant kind of ache that comes from actual productivity. My legs are sore from squatting to reach low drawers. My arms ache from lifting boxes, rearranging furniture, moving rugs. Yesterday was a full overhaul, closets emptied, linens sorted, drawers reorganized. Milly will be proud. I've got bags by the door for donation.

I throw on a short, white sundress and tie my hair up in a loose knot, eager to get some fresh air. I pass by Miss Paige's porch, where she's sipping coffee and reading a book. She waves with two fingers, and I wave back, comforted by the rhythm of the familiar.

Arthur's Bakery sits right in town. The white paint on the pineapple fence is fresh, a popular photo spot amongst tour-ists. Espresso and sugar lace the air from halfway down the block. The screen door shuts heavily as I step inside the air conditioning that's attempting to keep up with the summer heat. The glass cases are stocked with cinnamon rolls, donuts, and the infamous fruit pastries that always sell out by late morning.

I'm peering around the customer ordering ahead of me, scanning the pastry case for my favorite Danishes when I hear him say, "Let's do the rest of the cheese Danishes, as well."

My head snaps up and I let out an audible gasp. Notebook Guy spins around, startled by the sound.

I feel my face heat as I stare up at him, frozen. He's taller than I remembered, and up close, the creases around his deep green eyes crinkle with quiet amusement. They're like polished emeralds, bright, intense, mesmerizing. His sun-kissed skin has that effortless glow, and dark, shaggy waves frame his face. There's a trace of scruff along his jawline that's far too distracting this early in the morning.

Notebook Guy laughs, low, warm, and confident. "Or is that a bad idea?"

"Oh. No, I mean…" I fumble. "They're one of the best things on the island. You really can't go wrong with anything here."

I tack that last part on too fast, too bright.

His eyes crinkle again, charming satisfaction spreading across his face. He knows exactly how off balance I am.

He turns back to the counter. "Actually, I'll just take two of the cheese Danishes. And throw in four sticky buns, please."

Meanwhile, my face flushes as I pretend to dig through my purse, hands fumbling like I'm searching for something important instead of spiraling into full blown panic. That's when I hear it.

"Yeah the system is down so we can only take cash today." Damn. I don't have any cash on me. My brain scrambles through my options: stand here like a clueless idiot, ask a complete stranger to cover me, or vanish.

I choose vanish. Quietly, I inch backward toward the door, praying he doesn't notice me slipping out. But the screen door betrays me with a loud slam. I don't look back. I just walk. Fast. Flustered. I head toward home, pride left somewhere back on the bakery floor. A couple minutes later I hear the soft rumble of a golf cart pulling up beside me.

"I thought you said these were the best on the island?"

I glance over. There he is, grinning from the driver's seat, leaning against the steering wheel, two oversized white boxes sitting beside him.

"Was I just pastry hustled? Why'd you disappear?"

I snort before I can stop myself. So much for salvaging my dignity.

"I wasn't hustling you," I say, smiling despite myself. "They really are my favorite. I just forgot cash." I lift my hands in a helpless shrug.

His grin widens. "Well lucky for you, I'm a generous guy. And…" he nods toward the boxes, "I clearly went a little overboard. My friends won't miss a few."

Then he pats the seat next to him, eyebrows raised in invitation. I glance around. It's not even eight thirty in the morning on a very public street. If this is how I get murdered, at least it'll be carb adjacent.

"Why not," I shrug, circling the cart and climbing in. He watches me settle, a smug smile on his face.

"I promise this is strictly breakfast related," he says, deadpan, pulling the cart off to the side.

"I'm trusting you," I reply.

"Okay." He pops open a box with flourish. Inside, golden perfection. "Let's see if these live up to the hype."

I pretend to hesitate, then snatch one. He grabs his own and tucks the box between us.

"Moment of truth," he says, locking eyes with me. He takes a massive bite, flakes falling on his lap, his shirt, one sticking to his eyelash.

He groans. "Okay. You weren't lying. Totally worth it."

I dive into mine, messy and unapologetic. "I'd never lie about something this important."

He brushes crumbs off his shirt, failing miserably. "Let's just stay here and eat the rest. I'll tell my friends the bakery sold out."

I grin, my heart fluttering.

After a beat, I extend a buttery hand. "I'm Lucy, by the way."

"Noah." He takes it, grip lingering a second longer than necessary.

"So, Noah," I say, pulling back, "what brings you to the island? Besides picking up strangers on the side of the road."

"I'm working with a local musician," he says. "I'm here for a couple months."

"You're a musician?"

"Songwriter. I'm helping Jacob Alistair with his next album."

My eyebrows lift. "He's good. He played at a Christmas party I went to last year."

"He is," Noah agrees, then looks at me. "What about you?"

I hesitate. "My grandparents had a house here. I've been visiting since I was a kid."

His eyes light up. He throws an arm out, gesturing around us. "You grew up with this? I'm jealous."

"It's pretty special," I admit.

He stares at me intently. "I saw you at Gusty's the other night."

"You did," I confirm with a laugh. "First day back."

"Some friends of mine are in town this week. We're having dinner at the house they're renting tonight. You should come by. There'll be music, drinks, nothing wild."

I glance at him, trying to read the vibe. "I'd like that. I could probably come by after dinner. Where's the house?"

"It's White Cottage, on the Bay."

"I know it. It's next to a family friend's place."

Before I can say more, a golf cart rumbles up beside us. Jack.

"Hey Luce," he calls, smiling, eyes flicking between Noah and me.

"Morning, Jack," I say lightly, eyeing the bag next to him. "How are you?"

"Good. The boat came in. Finally got the extension cord I needed." He glances at Noah and nods. "Hey, I'm Jack."

"Noah," he replies, offering a smile. "Nice to meet you."

An awkward pause hovers. I can feel Jack's curiosity, Noah's calm, and me, stuck in the middle.

"Well," I say, rising. "I should head home."

"I'm going that way," Jack says, voice a little lower than usual.

I turn to Noah. "Thanks for breakfast. And not murdering me."

"Anytime," he replies. "Maybe I'll see you tonight. Bring a friend if you want."

"Maybe you will," I say, stepping off the cart with half a sticky bun in hand.

"See ya later, Lucy," he calls as he drives off.

I climb into Jack's cart, brushing pastry flakes off my dress. He pulls away smoothly, glancing over with a crooked smile.

"New friend?"

I laugh, easing into the seat. "Something like that."

"Did he lure you in with food?"

"One cheese Danish and a sticky bun," I say, holding up my half-eaten proof.

As we drive home, an uncomfortable silence builds between us. I look over and Jack has an uncharacteristic frown pulling down the corners of his mouth.

I hesitate and then ask, "You okay?"

"Of course. You sharing?" Jack smiles as he leans toward me.

I hold out the sticky bun. He leans in and takes a bite like it's the most normal thing in the world.

"I have a few things to do back at the house this morning before my parents get in. You know how mom likes her palms."

Every summer Jack, Allie, and I would comb the island for his mother's vases like it was some sacred mission. Jack hopping out every few minutes to snip a palm frond. There's no flower shop on the island, so you have to get creative.

"Then you could probably use a little sustenance," I say as I offer the rest of my sticky bun.

He chews, grinning, and I can't help but grin back, the tension melting between us.

Chapter Five

THAT EVENING, DAWN AND I ARE PERCHED AT THE END OF THE BAR at The Dunmore, a chic, celebrity-favorite boutique hotel on the island. It's located right on the beach, and the Amanda Lindroth-designed restaurant glimmers in that just-right lived in way, where everything looks a little warmer, everyone a little prettier. Lively conversation and clinking glasses buzz around us. I've convinced her to come with me tonight, even though "some stranger's party" might be stretching the definition of an enticing invite.

I'm wearing a chocolate brown silk tank dress that skims my body and hits just above my knees, with a U-shape neckline that dips low enough to feel thrilling but not trying too hard. Before leaving, I dug through Gran's jewelry box and found a long turquoise pendant necklace that compliments the dress. I feel good.

Dawn takes a sip of her drink, then runs an approving glance over my dress with a knowing smirk.

"Remind me why we're crashing this mystery man's party again?"

I roll my eyes even as a smile tugs at my lips. "It's not crashing if we were invited. Albeit loosely."

She tilts her head. "Define loosely."

I glance around, momentarily unsure. The vibe here feels cozy, safe. "We could just stay here. These are arguably the best seats in the house."

Dawn leans forward, resting a hand on the bar in front of me. "No, I was just teasing. And definitely not when you look this good and this guy is supposedly that hot. We're going, I'm totally vetting this Noah."

I sigh, swirling what's left of my Rum Dum. "He probably thinks Jack is my boyfriend after this morning. And I'm sure he noticed me with him at Gusty's."

"All the more reason to show up and set the record straight. Besides, a little distraction might be just what you need."

I chew on my lip. "I'm not falling into old patterns with Jack."

Dawn tsks, eyes twinkling. "No one would blame you if you did. But still, you owe it to yourself to show up and see what happens."

I take a deep breath, letting her words settle. "Yeah, you're right."

She clinks her glass against mine with a twinkle in her eye. "I always am."

On the way to the party we take the long route through town to calm my nerves. Dawn's golf cart zips along Bay Street as we pass kids on bikes, tourists strolling from dinner to drinks in linen pants and resort dresses, the late evening golden and still buzzing.

When we pull up at White Cottage, I'm immediately struck by how beautifully the property unfolds. The main house, two guest cottages nestled into the lush landscape, and even a newly built pickleball court at the far end.

We follow a coral stone path lined with flickering wicker lanterns, the warm glow casting playful shadows across the walkway.

"We're absolutely staying longer than planned," Dawn whispers, nudging me.

Rounding the corner, the backyard spills out before us, string lights zigzagging overhead, the long candlelit table still dotted with abandoned water glasses, their sides dripping into the tablecloth. A local band plays in the corner, filling the air with a cover of "Linger" by the Cranberries while a few people dance barefoot on the grass. To the right, a cozy fire pit area glows softly, and I immediately spot Noah. He's sitting with a small group but glancing around distractedly. When his eyes find mine, his whole face lights up.

As he stands, I take him in. Noah's in a sand-colored linen shirt, the sleeves rolled to his forearms, the top few buttons undone. Loose but tailored pants, bare ankles, salt seemingly still in his hair. He looks like someone who never has to try, the kind of cool that comes from being comfortable everywhere.

"You made it," he says warmly, his hands diving into his pockets like he's not sure what else to do with them.

"It seems I did." My smile gives me away as we hold each other's gaze, that now familiar flutter in my stomach unfurling low and insistent.

After a beat he turns to Dawn. "Hi, I'm Noah."

"Dawn," she says, extending a hand. "I'm the chaperone, just in case you were indeed a murderer," she winks.

"I'm glad someone has her back," he laughs, then looks back at me. "Want to meet everyone?"

We move through the backyard. The group around the fire pit shifts as we join, and Noah begins introducing us.

"This is Lucy and Dawn," he says.

"Welcome," a tall guy with a mess of curly hair extends a hand. "Hello Lucy-who-we-thought-Noah-made-up. I'm Miguel."

I laugh, feeling instantly at ease. A beautiful brunette slips into the circle with a smile like sunlight.

"This is Kate," Noah says, gesturing between us. "Kate, Lucy and Dawn."

"So you are real," Kate says, eyes shimmering. "It's nice to meet you."

"Should I be concerned that everyone thought you made me up?" I laugh, glancing at him.

"Not at all," he deadpans as the rest of the group laughs. He throws a quick wink my way that sends a shiver down my spine.

"Don't mind him," Kate squeezes his shoulder. "Better watch yourself, Noah. She's going to hear all your secrets by the end of the night."

"Guess I'd better keep her distracted," he says smoothly, then turns to Dawn and me. "Can I get you something?"

"Wine would be great," I say.

"I'm good," Dawn says, somehow already holding a wine glass.

"Want to follow me?" Noah asks, and of course, I do.

Inside, the kitchen is winding down. The catering team moves in quiet efficiency, trays being packed, glasses stacked with military precision. He leads me to a tucked away wet bar beneath a row of open shelves, the glow of the underlighting wrapping the space in a warm, golden haze.

He scans the bottles, then plucks one without hesitation. "Baby Sancerre okay?"

"Perfect," I say, watching as he carefully chooses a thin-rimmed glass and pours. He hands me one, then lifts his own, tilting it toward me.

"To our what…fifth encounter?"

I laugh, meeting his gaze as our glasses clink. "Good to know you're keeping track."

His smile turns slow. "Hard not to."

"I agree," I say, smiling into my drink.

A beat stretches between us.

He breaks it first. "Alright, real question for a local. Why do people call Harbour Island Briland?"

"Say Harbour Island five times fast." I grin.

He tries, stumbles, then laughs as the syllables collapse. "Ahhh, Briland. I get it."

"You said you're here working on an album. How long have you been here?"

"Since mid-May, but I left for a few days last weekend to take a meeting back home."

"So other than driving on the opposite side of the road," I bump my arm against his, "you've probably gotten the hang of things around here. What do you think?"

He tips his head, weighing the question, before his voice lowers conspiratorially. "That coconut at Vic-Hum is definitely getting bigger. I feel like it's training for something."

My shoulders shake as I laugh at his unexpected declaration. "Yeah, hard to believe it's the largest coconut in the world though."

"It is. But this island is great, to answer your question. I love the people, and the laid-back vibe. I miss my Whole Foods though," he says, taking a sip before tilting his head toward me. "So, what's your controversial island opinion?"

I frown. "Excuse me?"

"You know…like, 'conch salad is overrated,' or 'nobody actually likes Goombay Smashes.' Something mildly controversial."

I grin. "Okay. Let's see…well, I actually *don't* like Goombay Smashes," I say, tilting my glass to him. "But I'm the rare exception. But also…everyone here is only pretending they don't like karaoke night."

He throws his head back, laughing. "Well don't worry, I won't pretend that I don't."

"Your turn," I challenge, twitching my lips.

"There's always one guy in a pink shirt who swears he discovered the island," Noah says without missing a beat.

"So true," I exclaim. My brain stalls, cursor blinking, searching for something clever to say, before squinting my eyes back at Noah.

"If you've never showered by candlelight during a power outage you haven't earned your stripes."

I realize a second too late how that sounds. Noah's grin falters into something crooked, like my answer tugged it off course. His eyes darken and stay locked on mine. The kitchen seems to narrow until it's just the two of us, the chatter and laughter outside thinning to a dull buzz. The only thing sharp is the glow of the light between us, the faint clink of glassware as the caterers finish up.

"I've totally cornered you, haven't I?"

"I don't mind," I say and mean it.

"Still." He straightens a little. "Don't want Dawn to worry."

He starts to step away, then pauses, looking back at me with a spark in his eyes. "Unless you've got another dramatic exit planned."

Heat rushes to my face as the bakery this morning flashes back, and I don't hate it.

Back outside, we drift toward the fire pit. Dawn is mid-story, making Kate laugh with her whole body. She's in her element, animated hands, quick wit, all of it.

"Looks like your friend's found her people," Noah says, brushing against me as we sit.

"All people are Dawn's people," I reply. As I settle in, he subtly adjusts a pillow behind me.

"So," Miguel says, leaning forward, "Noah mentioned you grew up coming here?"

"I did." I nod. "My grandparents had a house on the island. I've spent every summer and most Christmases here. I'm from Charleston, South Carolina, though."

"Jealous," says Jess, a petite brunette with a big, warm smile. "That sounds like the dream."

"I went to a wedding in Charleston last spring," Noah adds next to me. "Only had a day, but I wandered the historic district. Beautiful city."

"Yeah, it has a way of pulling you back. I left for college, but I couldn't stay away."

"What do you do there?" Kate asks.

"I'm an artist, I have a studio downtown."

"I'd love to see your work," Noah says.

Conversation drifts to cities, music, family quirks. Kate's celebrating her thirtieth birthday, and Miguel explains that they all met in college. The group is warm and easy, the kind of creative people who open up fast and make space for everyone. Someone tops off drinks.

At some point I realize Noah and I have leaned closer. Our legs brush repeatedly. He doesn't pull away. Neither do I.

Later, when the music fades and I notice Kate yawning, I catch Dawn's eye, sharing a look. The silent communication we've perfected over the years.

"We should probably head out," I say, standing and thanking everyone for welcoming us.

"Glad you came," Miguel says, rising with the others. "Let's plan something again before we leave."

As we head toward the driveway, Dawn leans in to air kiss Noah goodbye, then tosses me a look, the kind that says *take your time*, before peeling off toward the golf cart.

He and I take the lantern lit path as slowly as we can, palm fronds whispering overhead, our steps falling into sync. Just before we reach the driveway, Noah slows to a stop.

He turns to me with a crooked smile. "You made tonight a lot better."

"You make that sound like it wasn't already good."

"It wasn't this good." He holds my gaze for a beat before sliding his hands into his pockets and continuing. "Can I see you again?"

"I think I could be convinced," I smile.

He tilts his head, considering. "Should I text you tomorrow? Or wait the standard seventy-two hours?"

"If you wait seventy-two hours, I'll forget your name."

"Well, I'm not letting that happen," he says, already pulling out his phone.

Our screens glow side by side in the lantern light as we trade numbers. His thumb hovers just a second longer before he hits save, and the moment feels oddly suspended, like something small that matters more than it should.

"Goodnight, Lucy," he says softly, and it feels like possibility.

Chapter Six

I'M PERCHED ON THE COUNTER IN DAWN'S BOUTIQUE, BRILAND Bloom, flipping through a copy of Graham Vale's photography book *Leisure Class*. The space smells faintly of salt and sandalwood—linen dresses, raffia bags, stacks of coffee table books, and handmade jewelry lining the pale pink shelves.

Dawn's family goes way back on Harbour Island. They run the ferry business down at the dock, but she built this shop from scratch. We met as kids, two barefoot girls running around the sand roads.

I flip to a photo taken here on the island. Pink sand, a wicker umbrella, a woman laughing beside a man with a camera. "Harbour Island, 1965," the caption reads.

"Do you think these were real people or models?"

Dawn shrugs. "Probably both. You know how it was back then. Everyone wanted to be in front of Graham Vale's lens. Apparently, half the island girls were in love with him back in the day."

"Can you blame them?" I say, flipping another page. "He looked like he belonged in his own photos."

Graham Vale's work is practically island wallpaper. Every house has a copy of *Leisure Class* somewhere. He was *the* photographer from the sixties through the early 2000s, famous for capturing the rich and sunburned looking effortlessly undone. Half the photos in this book were shot on Harbour Island. He still owns a house on the bay, though no one ever sees him.

"It would be cool if you could get Graham to sign these books, you know?"

"Sure, that would be brilliant. But how? He's a hermit now. I'm not even sure the last time he was on the island. So," she continues, focused on steaming the cotton gauze dress in front of her, "do you want to unpack last night with Noah, or are you still mentally replaying it on a loop?"

"I'm not mentally replaying anything."

"Of course you're not," she says, flicking the steamer off and turning toward me. "You were literally beaming when you walked up to the golf cart last night."

I glance down at my phone, the notification still sitting there.

> **Noah:** Last night was fun. Let me know if you're free this weekend.

I reread it then flip the phone over.

"He's nice," I say carefully. "Very easy to like."

"And yet, you haven't texted him back."

"I will, I just…want to breathe it all in. I just got here. I'm still recalibrating."

Dawn rolls her eyes. "You've had one spontaneous golf cart moment and a few flirty wine toasts. He's not proposing."

"I know," I laugh. "But it's not about him. It's about me not jumping into something just because it feels good."

She studies me for a beat, then nods. "That's fair. *If* that's why."

"The season *is* just beginning," Dawn continues, unpacking a stack of dresses from another delivery box. "Everyone's starting to arrive."

"I think Allie gets in today." There's something about that first wave of arrivals, like summer's officially started once we're all back together again.

She glances at me. "And Jack?"

I pause, closing the book and stacking it next to the others. "I mean, we've obviously seen each other a few times," I say noncommittally.

The rustle of tissue paper fills the silence while Dawn keeps unpacking, deliberate and steady.

"It's weird," I admit. "Being around him. It's like my body remembers things before my brain catches up. We fall into this easy rhythm, like nothing's changed, but of course everything has."

"Has it been hard? Finally seeing him?"

I nod. "Not in the way I thought it would be. Just…confusing. He's still Jack, even though it's been two years. But I don't know what version of *me* I'm supposed to be with him anymore."

Dawn shakes her head and sighs. "I still can't believe you guys broke up."

I chew on my bottom lip. "We live different lives except when we're here. When Jack's in New York, everything is measured by how loud your ambition is. He turns into a person consumed by the next promotion, the next big deal, as if he has to prove himself to anyone and everyone."

My throat tightens as I run my fingers across a shell picture frame. "I've never doubted him, but that wasn't enough."

"I used to fly up on weekends, and we'd squeeze each other into forty-eight hours between client dinners and flights. And every Sunday night, right before I left, he'd promise things would calm down. They never did."

I can't stop because I don't think I've ever said any of this out loud. "He kept building this tower higher and higher because he thought that's where security lived. But there was no room left for me. For us. And the thing is," I add, softer, "I never felt at home up there. The city's exciting, sure, but I always felt like I was borrowing someone else's world when I visited. I'd leave and feel so relieved."

Dawn exhales, nodding. "You've always been an open air and barefoot kind of girl."

"Exactly." I smile, a little sad. "But Jack thinks he needs the skyscrapers."

"Well, you know I'm always team Lucy," Dawn smiles at me. "He does seem different this summer, though. Don't you think?"

"Maybe. I guess he does seem more relaxed, less guarded. Almost like the guy I fell in love with."

After I leave Dawn's shop, I steer the Jolly down to the Customs building on Government dock, a modest structure with peeling pink paint and a perpetually spinning fan. After I sign the logbook, the attendant disappears to retrieve my shipment.

"Lucy?"

I turn to see Helen from the art gallery approaching.

"I thought I saw you driving the Jolly the other day. Are you picking up house supplies?" She asks, giving me a hug hello.

I shake my head. "Art supplies, actually. Hopefully every-thing made it."

"I'd love to see what you're working on."

"If I ever get started," I laugh. "But I'll come by the gallery soon. I saw you have a new Amos Ferguson painting that I'm dying to see in person."

Her eyes brighten. "Swing by this week, I'll make sure you get the full tour."

After I unpack my paints at the house, I drag the easel out onto the back porch, the old boards warm beneath my bare feet. The shade from the house, along with the breeze off the ocean, keeps me cool enough in the afternoon heat. I queue up the *Folklore* album and squeeze dollops of blues and greens onto my palette. I layer strokes across the canvas, letting the water take shape. The curve of the waves, the shadows in the sand, the weightless sweep of clouds. I'm not painting any-thing exact, just trying to capture a feeling.

Time blurs in the best way. Starting a fresh canvas, I pull in more color this time, dipping my brush into a rich lilac. It's the first time I've felt pulled toward a blank canvas in weeks, maybe months. Back home, I'd been stuck in a loop of com-missions, everything careful and boxed in. Here, it's looser. The colors want to move again, and I finally want to follow them. My phone rattles on the arm of the porch chair.

Allie: You home? Come over, we have snacks and a baby!

I grin. It's the kind of interruption I welcome, and it pulls me out of my trance.

I slip on my sandals and walk the two doors over, spotting Allie on the porch swing, rocking Felix in a slow, hypnotic rhythm. The swing creaks, same as it did when we were kids swapping secrets, only now she's cradling a newborn instead of a box of Goldfish.

"There you are," she says softly, grinning as I step up onto the porch.

I lean in and kiss her cheek, peeking at Felix asleep in her arms. "How did you smuggle this angel onto the island?"

"Oh, it's a trick," she says, adjusting his sleeve with one hand. "He's like this just long enough to make me forget how tired I am before he turns into an eating machine."

I laugh and drop into the chair beside her. "How was the trip?"

"Not as easy as it used to be," she laughs. "I plan on doing absolutely nothing today except existing."

"I'll keep you company."

She tells me about the chaos of life with a new baby, her husband's refusal to pack anything until this morning, and how the only thing she's looking forward to more than wine is a nap.

"So," she says, tilting her head. "What's new with you?"

"I've just been settling in over at the house," I say, telling her about the plan to rent it out with Milly's help. "Between the two of us, she's definitely the one in charge. I think Gran trained her for this moment."

Allie laughs. "Your Gran could get a room full of grown men to move furniture with just a look."

For a second, we're both quiet, and I'm remembering how Gran would put us to work in the kitchen, the sound of her gold bangles clinking as she moved. It's nice to remember her like that, not just in the empty spaces she left behind.

Allie tilts her head. "How has it been seeing Jack? He mentioned you came over for margaritas."

"Yeah," I let out a slow breath. "We've seen each other a couple times." It's not untrue. But it leaves a lot unsaid. Allie and I have been close since we were kids, which makes the Jack of it all…complicated. She's had a front-row seat to every season of us.

Allie studies me for a beat longer, then leans back into the swing, her gaze softening.

"I'm glad," she says. "You two were always so close. I hate how weird it got there for a while."

I nod, my shoulders relaxing. "Yeah, me too."

When we take the baby down to the beach, Allie digs in the basket for a towel, and my gaze catches on one of Jack's old shirts, the cracked Harbour Island Sailing Club logo making my chest tighten.

I remember the summer I first ended up with it. Jack was helping with the sailing club, half counselor, half ringleader, and way too sure of himself. One of the campers was a kid I babysat, and I learned exactly how early I could arrive for pickup without looking obvious, parking myself in the same patch of shade.

One sweltering afternoon, he hauled a Sunfish sailboat out of the water and tugged his shirt over his head, skin slick with salt and sweat. He caught me watching and grinned, then tossed his shirt at me.

"Hold this before I melt."

It smelled like coconut sunscreen and sun. When he told me to keep it, I pretended it was nothing. But later that night, laying in bed, I replayed the moment over and over.

I wore it everywhere that summer, over my bikini, knotted at the waist with cutoffs, even once to the sailing club cookout, where he leaned in and teased, "Pretty sure it looks better on you, but don't tell the rest of the club." My stomach flipped, heat rushing to my face.

It's faded now, but one glimpse and I'm right back there, seventeen, sunburned, trying not to smile too big every time he looked my way.

Chapter Seven

Noah: Good morning Lucy
Noah: This is Noah by the way

I sit straight up in bed like I've just been given an adrenaline shot.

Lucy: Good morning
Noah: I almost texted you when I woke up but figured 6:23 might read as desperate
Lucy: You're right, waiting until 8:13 made all the difference
Noah: Exactly. It's the sweet spot between "I woke up thinking about you" and "Oh hey"

Okay, this is happening. My pulse speeds up as I race to think of a reply.

Lucy: Sorry I didn't get back to you yesterday. What are you up to?
Noah: Free as a bird. Breakfast?

We make plans to meet at The Landing. I jump out of bed and dart to my vanity, grateful to see it's a good hair day. I throw on low-waisted pale pink linen pants with a cropped white tank and comfy sandals so I can walk to the restaurant.

Twenty minutes later, I'm passing through the side gate of The Landing on Bay Street. I spot Noah leaning back in his chair with one arm slung over the side. When I reach the table, he stands, pulling out my chair.

"This table okay with you? They have space inside, too." he asks as he leans in.

"It's perfect. The porch is my favorite spot. I love watching everyone go by." I smile, setting my bag beside me on the chair. But as I glance around, a small realization hits. This looks like a date. And okay, fine. I think it actually is one. In all my years here, I've never been on a date on the island with anyone other than Jack. I scan the porch out of habit, but I don't recognize anyone.

We order right away, a latte and avocado toast with bacon for me, and a black iced coffee with ricotta pancakes for Noah.

Once the waitress walks away, Noah rests his elbows on the table. "So," he says, "I know you grew up splitting time. Charleston's home, and then summers here?"

"Pretty much," I nod. "Christmases, too. And sometimes Easter. It's always been like a second home to me."

His eyes stay on mine, his body still in that way people have when they're really listening. "And your art, did you always know you wanted to paint?"

I smile. "Always. I was the kid doodling on cocktail nap-kins at dinner parties and getting sand in my sketchbooks."

He tilts his head, appraising me with a soft smile playing on his lips. "You have that look of growing up around beauty. I guess you learned how to turn it into your own language."

My lips twitch into a smile before I can stop them. "That sounds like a songwriter."

He gives a small, sheepish shrug.

"Right…Nashville. And do you? Love what you do?"

"I do," his smile is easy. "It's mostly trying to get people to pay attention long enough to say or feel something true. Which is harder than it sounds."

I nod. "You make music sound a little like painting. Have you written anything I might've heard?"

He considers, then names one of my current favorite songs.

I blink. Hard. "Wait. You wrote that?!"

His ears turn slightly pink as he sips his coffee. "Co-wrote. It's all teamwork. But yeah."

"I love that song!" I practically shriek. "It's on my workout playlist. Sometimes I put it on repeat to help me get through a run."

He rubs the back of his neck, trying to play it off, but there's no mistaking the pleased twinkle in his eyes.

"Well, I'll take that as the highest compliment." Then his voice gets serious. "That's what I love about it, honestly. Taking a blank page and turning it into something people can feel. It's the best kind of high."

He takes another sip of his coffee, then meets my eyes. "You must get that. With painting?"

And I'm caught off guard. Not by the question itself, but by the fact that he asked it at all. The last couple of guys I went on first dates with could barely manage a follow-up question without cue cards.

I tell him about my studio, the women I share it with, how we share ideas, push each other, swap connections.

"It never gets competitive?" he asks.

"Not at all," I say, shaking my head. "There's this really supportive creative community in Charleston. Mostly women, a mix of artists, designers, brand founders. Everyone's always championing each other."

His head nods in quiet agreement. "That's how my writing crew is, too. The best stuff comes from that kind of energy and support."

I realize I'm leaning in closer than I mean to, caught up in the easy rhythm of our conversation. His laugh is quick, his questions thoughtful, and I keep catching myself fighting a grin that won't quit. When the check lands, he snatches it before I can even pretend to reach for it.

"Nope," he says, dismissing my halfhearted protest with a shake of his head.

I sigh, surrendering. "Thank you. Now I owe you breakfast."

His eyes flick up to mine. "Do you have some time? Want to go to the beach?" His tone sounds casual, but there's a slight hitch to it, like maybe he was nervous to ask. The invitation catches me off guard, but in the best way.

"I'd love to."

When we pull into my driveway, Noah slows the golf cart, his eyes sweeping up toward the house with a low whistle.

"Wow," he says, taking it in. "This is your grandparents' place?"

"It is," I say, then pause. "Well...was." I fiddle with the drawstring on my linen pants. "My grandmother passed away last month. She left it to me." I glance over at him. "It still feels weird to say out loud."

Noah turns to me, his whole demeanor softening. "I'm sorry, Lucy. It sounds like you were close?"

"Very," I nod. "She lived in Charleston, too, so we spent a lot of time together. But I feel better knowing she's with my grandfather now."

We ride in silence for a moment as the golf cart rolls over the shell-lined path. Noah doesn't rush to fill the quiet, which I appreciate.

He drums his fingers on the steering wheel as we stop near my gate. "I'll run home and grab my suit. I'll be right back?"

"Sounds good," I reply.

Fifteen minutes later, I'm just finishing tying the straps of my light pink bikini top when I hear the soft crunch of tires on the drive. I pause, fingers still, suddenly aware we'll be spending the day like this. I glance out the window.

Noah steps out of the golf cart like someone who's used to being barefoot. He's wearing navy swim trunks and the same white terry-cloth polo he wore at breakfast, a towel now slung over his shoulder. I flush, suddenly remembering that we're about to spend the day half-dressed together.

When I step onto the porch, he looks up, his attention settling on me.

"Let's grab some waters before we head down," I say, working to keep my voice breezy as I gesture for him to follow me inside.

In the kitchen, I grab two water bottles and start filling them with ice. Noah leans his hip against the counter.

"This house is incredible," he says. "All the light, the view. I don't know how you ever leave." Noah nods a thank you as I pass him a bottle.

"Thanks. I'm hoping to spend more time here. I'm turning one of the upstairs rooms into a little studio space while I'm here."

I continue, twisting the lid on my water bottle. "I've never painted seascapes before, as an adult I mean. They always felt a little too obvious…" I gesture out the window. "But now, I don't know. I've been feeling it."

We head outside, passing under the arbor onto the pink, sandy path.

"This is a painting in and of itself," Noah murmurs behind me, taking in the framed view of the bougainvillea crawling over the arbor with the turquoise water right beyond it.

The breeze curls softly around us as we step onto the beach. I lead him toward the chairs tucked near the dune, and we drag them under the palapa, tossing our towels over the backs. I nudge my chair just a few inches closer to his. If he notices, he doesn't say anything. We settle in, the sun warm on our skin, and for the next few hours the conversation flows like we've done this before. Noah's sharp, witty in a quiet way that sneaks up on me. And he's a great listener.

Also, God help me, he's hot. When he took his shirt off, I scolded myself to stop staring. He's tall with tanned skin, his stomach is toned and lean, and there's an ease to the way he moves, like someone shaped by late nights, heavy instruments, and hours lost in music, not fluorescent-lit gyms. There's nothing staged about it. Just lived-in strength. He stretches his arms above his head, muscles shifting, and lets out a low, satisfied sigh.

"This might be the best way to spend a day off," he says, eyes closed.

"I thought musicians didn't have days off?"

He cracks one eye open, smirking. "Everyone needs a day off. I'm calling this a creative reset."

"Ah. So this is part of your *process*."

"Fully sanctioned," he says, looking over at me. "Beach, good company, maybe a little inspiration…all very necessary."

I shake my head, smiling. "So if I hear a song one day about a mysterious island girl…"

"You'll know exactly who it's about."

It's like a brushstroke of color blooming under my ribs.

Hours later, I'm lying on my side, laughing as I tell Noah about my middle school notebooks, pages of dramatic, painfully sincere poems I once believed were masterpieces.

His mouth drops open, amused disbelief flickering across his face. "No way. I have to see these."

"Absolutely not," I say, swatting his arm. "They are deeply embarrassing and will never, ever see daylight."

He leans in closer, eyes glinting. "Come on. I won't judge. Maybe I could turn one into a ballad."

I groan. "I'd die if my middle school angst ended up on the radio."

"I used to spend hours illustrating and decorating the borders," I confess, peeking out behind my raised hands. "Dramatic flourishes, swirling designs, extremely intense titles in all-caps bubble letters."

"Bubble letters?" he repeats, delighted.

"With shading," I add quickly. "I was very committed."

His gaze lingers before he looks away. I flop onto my back, laughing up at the sky. God, I haven't felt like this in a while, light, flushed, a little unsteady in the best way.

My stomach growls loud enough to make us both laugh again, and we head up to the house in search of food.

"Okay, you're in luck," I announce, pulling a chilled bowl from the fridge. "Milly makes the best chicken salad you'll ever have."

Noah leans over my shoulder, close enough that I catch the salt-sweet trace of the ocean clinging to his skin. "I have to meet this Milly."

"She's a saint. And she's a magician in the kitchen."

I scoop generous spoonfuls onto slices of fresh bread from Arthur's Bakery and slide a plate toward him.

One bite in, he groans, tipping his head back. "Oh, yeah. This is life changing."

I catch a flash of movement through the front window. Jack, kneeling in the grass beside Milly, tugging at a stray vine along the fence, piling it neatly at his side. She's chatting, hands flying the way they do, and he's listening and nodding.

Something tightens low in my chest, followed quickly by a puzzled irritation. Why is Jack in my yard?

I look away before Noah can follow my gaze. "Told you it's good."

He sets the sandwich down for a moment, scanning the shelves, the bits and pieces of home that make up this kitchen. His gaze lands on a sketch hung on the side of the fridge, the ink faded around the edges.

"Did you draw this?" he asks, reaching toward it but not touching.

I study the quick line sketch I'd done many years ago. A self-portrait, laughing on the beach, sun-streaked hair flying in the wind. It's been there for years, familiar to the point of invisibility.

"Yeah," I say, suddenly self-conscious. "Just a doodle."

Noah shakes his head, eyes still on it. "That's not *just* anything." And the way he says it makes me shift on my feet, embarrassed but warmed.

I glance out the window one last time and can't help but bristle. Jack's still there with Milly, pruning my plants like it's his yard, like he's always belonged here.

When I turn back around, I notice Noah's gaze had followed mine.

"Is that Jack?" he asks. "You two…close?"

The question punches a tiny hole in my composure. I force a shrug, hoping it lands somewhere between casual and unbothered.

"We dated a long time ago," I say lightly. "It's…nothing."

Nothing. Sure. If nothing is a small electric shock every time I see him.

Noah nods once, slow, watching me more than the window. He doesn't press, but I'm suddenly furious that Jack hovering in my yard is ruining this moment. I reach for my water like I'm totally fine.

"Ready to head back down to the beach?" I ask, too brightly.

"Lead the way."

When Noah and I settle into our beach chairs again, they're somehow even closer than before. I swear I only scooted mine once, but now our arms could brush if either of us shifted an inch.

A little after five, Noah's phone buzzes. "Mind if I grab this?"

"Of course not." I stretch my legs in the sand as he answers, his voice sliding into that deeper register men save for phone calls, each word drawn out just a touch more. It's a quick conversation, and when he hangs up, he turns back to me.

"That was Miguel. There's an impromptu pickleball tournament happening back at their house. Apparently everyone's been drinking, so I'm guessing the stakes are low."

His lips curl up, playful. "Want to be my partner?"

"You mean right now?" I ask, sitting up.

"Yeah. But only if you want. I don't mind skipping it."

I rise, brushing sand from my legs with an exaggerated sigh. "Only if you're prepared to win."

Noah laughs as I take off toward the house. Upstairs, I pull out my white pleated tennis skirt and matching sports top. It's cute. A little flirty. I catch myself smiling as I tie my hair up.

When I get back downstairs, Noah's waiting in the doorway. His eyes sweep over me slowly, lingering just long enough that my stomach tightens.

"Damn," he says, lips quirking. "You're not messing around."

I brush past him with a grin. "Hope you can keep up, Nashville."

He falls in step beside me, laughing. "Not gonna lie, you're a little intimidating."

I wink, ponytail swinging. "Good."

On the way, we swing by Noah's rental so he can change. While he jogs inside, I linger by the cart, eyeing the house with its teal shutters and sun-faded siding. Music drifts faintly from somewhere inside, and through the front window I catch a glimpse of a couple guitars propped in the corner. The whole place feels like a cross between a summer hideaway and a creative den.

When he reappears, fresh T-shirt, hair pushed back, he doesn't hesitate to reach for my hand, and I feel it with my whole body.

By the time we pull up to White Cottage, everyone is already gathered. Light spills over the pickleball court, making the whole scene warm and cinematic.

"Oh my God, Lucy, that is the *cutest* pickleball outfit!" Kate shouts, practically skipping toward me.

I laugh, instantly relieved by her warmth, my nerves about crashing their group again dissolving.

"Thanks, Kate," I grin, tightening my ponytail. "I can't believe this house has its own court."

"I know, right?" She leans in, lowering her voice. "Also? Just so you know, original plan was boys versus girls, but Noah insisted on being your partner."

I poorly attempt a neutral expression. "Oh, really?"

Kate's grin widens, all mischief.

"Hmmm, I think we girls need to stick together. Let's do this."

Kate squeals and spins back toward the court. "We switched up the teams," she announces. "It's girls versus boys."

Noah's eyes find mine instantly, checking for any hint of protest. I stick out my tongue, playfully, a warm rush blooming in my chest again. Miguel arrives with a tray of champagne flutes, floating across the court like a waiter in a resort ad.

"If you break a glass, you're automatically docked two points," he says solemnly before breaking into a grin.

I raise my glass. "It's safe with me."

We all toast before Kate pulls me toward the court. We're up first against Noah and Miguel. I'm a solid player thanks to semi-regular practice with friends at home. And luckily Kate and I click easily, both quick and focused, both a little too competitive to pretend otherwise.

Noah, meanwhile, is still piecing it together. It's honestly adorable watching him pause mid-play to double check the rules, lips quirking as he mutters, "Wait, was that in?" He's naturally athletic, though, and it evens out his inexperience.

Miguel's a total ringer. Apparently he played tennis in college, and the match stays tight. The vibe is rowdy and unserious, trash talk flying, Kate christening us *Bahama Lobs*, Noah taking dramatic dives just to make us laugh.

"Hope you boys don't mind losing," Kate says, bouncing the ball with a wicked grin.

She serves. The rally's quick, sharp, relentless. We're zipping across the court, calling shots, slipping into a rhythm like we've played together for years. My pulse hammers, sweat trickling down my neck, hair sticking to my skin. But I don't care. A fast return rockets straight at me. I pivot and whip a backhand cross-court. It zips past Noah's paddle, landing clean.

"Game!" Kate and I shriek, paddles high, jumping into a ridiculous little victory circle. She does a spin. I nearly trip over my own feet.

Noah taps my paddle. "We're going to need a rematch, preferably before Miguel disowns me as a partner."

"Dang, Lucy," Miguel says. "You've got a killer backhand. Remind me not to trash talk you next round."

Noah grins at me over the net, curls damp, eyes dancing. "You've been holding out on me, Briland."

I shrug, feigning innocence. "Have to keep you on your toes."

As we step off the court, we drift toward the table where our waters wait, letting the others rotate in. The air is thick with the humid haze of evening, sweat lingering on my skin. I towel off, take a slow sip, and try not to notice the heat of Noah beside me, close enough that every inch of space feels charged. When I glance up, he's staring at me with an unnerving intensity.

"Today's been so fun," I say, voice soft as I lean back against the fence.

He tips his chin downward, resting his hand on top of the fence beside me. "Yeah. It has."

I bump his shoulder lightly. "You weren't half-bad out there."

His grin turns sly. "Not 'half-bad'?"

I tilt my head, pretending to consider, lips tugging into a teasing half smile. Before I can answer, he steps forward, hand reaching out to tip my chin up, a question in his eyes. I don't even think, just nod, and he closes the distance with the softest brush of a kiss, gentle and teasing.

I melt against him, our skin damp with the salt and sun of the day. His arms are strong and certain, and the sounds of the match blur behind us. For a breathless beat I feel anchored, like the world has narrowed to this exact patch of court, this exact moment.

Chapter Eight

"LUCE?" DAWN'S VOICE FLOATS UP THE STAIRS.

"Up here," I call, hearing the front door slam shut. I'm standing in front of my closet, wrapped in a towel, considering the dress in my hands.

She appears a moment later, her box braids twisted into a loose knot, looking effortlessly cool in a sheer black dress.

"Tell me you've finally narrowed it down," she says, flopping onto my bed.

I level her with a look. "Does this *seem* narrowed down?"

Dawn's eyes flick over the chaos of clothing draped across the chair, the closet door, the bed. "So…no."

She crosses her legs, leaning back like she has all night. "We've got time. You just need to find the one that says, 'effortlessly gorgeous,' and 'no, I'm not new here.'"

I laugh. "That's a lot of work for one dress."

"It's the Farrows' summer party," she says, like that's a universally understood concept. "Everyone who's back on the island will be there."

I nod, sipping from my glass of water. "I know."

She studies me for a second too long, then grins. "Okay, now tell me why you're glowing. What have I missed?"

I try to keep my face neutral, but my mouth betrays me. I'm already smiling.

"I hung out with Noah all day yesterday."

Dawn sits upright. "Like…all day?"

"Breakfast, then the beach, then pickleball, maybe a kiss. Yep."

Her eyes widen. "Oh my God! And how are we feeling about him now?"

I laugh, tugging a silky green Doen dress off the hanger. "It was really fun. He's so easy to be around. I mean, you met him. He's just cool."

Dawn leans forward. "You like him."

I hold up the green dress between us like a shield. "No comment."

"But yeah. I like him." I squeal, curling my hands up to my neck.

She grins. "Well damn. Looks like we're entering a new era."

"Maybe. It just…it doesn't feel like a thing I have to figure out. It just is."

Dawn resumes leaning back on her hands, satisfied. "Good. You deserve easy. You deserve fun."

I smile, holding up the dress. "You think I should wear this one?"

She tilts her head, considering. "It's hot. But try that white one with the open back."

I pull the white dress from where it's been hanging on the back of the closet door and hold it up. "Okay, this could actually be the one."

"Yeah she is," Dawn says, beaming. "Is Allie riding with us?"

"No, she's gotta put Felix down first."

The drive to the party is quick as we wind softly through narrow, palm-lined roads. When we pull up, the Farrows' house is like a movie set, soft light spilling through open shuttered windows and doors, lanterns strung from tree to tree, flickering gently in the breeze. Music drifts from the coral stone terraces, threaded with laughter and the clink of glassware.

The Farrows always host the first *real* party of the summer. Their daughter, Sloane, is one of those friends who's more like chosen family after endless summers diving off boats together. The first time I met her was on the beach when we were both nine. I had seen her around the island before but was too shy to say hello. I was walking down the beach on a quest for shells, and Sloane had set up a table on the beach in front of her house selling beaded jewelry that she'd made that summer. By that afternoon I was helping her make bracelets. Now Sloane is an art dealer in New York with clients all over the world.

Inside, the party buzzes with unmistakable Harbour Island energy: partly glamorous, partly relaxed, zinging with the quiet thrill of summer officially beginning. Familiar faces float through the rooms in resort wear. Friends catch up like no time has passed. It's the kind of crowd that knows each other's stories but still leans in like they're hearing them for the first time.

Dawn and I make our way through the comfortable mix of locals, returning second homeowners, and the occasional too-famous-to-stare-at celebrity. The island has a way of level-ing the playing field. We snag two flutes of champagne from a passing tray and are halfway through the great room, scanning for Sloane, when I hear my name.

"Lucy. Darling Dawn."

I turn to find Mrs. Farrow, elegant as ever in a gold, silk embroidered caftan, bangles sliding up her arm, gliding toward us with a welcoming smile.

"Hi, Mrs. Farrow," I say, leaning in for a cheek kiss.

"You look beautiful, sweetheart. You and that flawless complexion, I swear you get more luminous as the years tick by," she says with a wink. "Dawn, thank you again for saving me this morning with this dress."

"You hardly needed saving, Mrs. Farrow. But you know I always love dressing you."

"You do look beautiful. As is this party," I say, looking around at the servers weaving through the crowd in crisp linen, the women in pale pink shift dresses, the men in match-ing shirts and white trousers, graceful despite their polished pace. "It gets more impressive every year."

The Farrows' estate stretches along the beach, its white-washed walls glowing against the night. French doors open to the breeze, revealing a great room lined with white coral stone and towering palms in blue-and-white urns. Hundreds of candles flicker in hurricane glass, mirrored by the reflection of the pool outside, a sheet of turquoise framed by bougainvil-lea and white umbrellas that still haven't been folded, even as night settles in. Somewhere near the veranda, a jazz trio winds through an island version of "Dream a Little Dream of Me."

She waves a hand, brushing off the compliment, though she's clearly pleased. "We love this party. It's not really summer until everyone's under this roof with a glass in hand. Are your parents here this year?"

I shake my head. "Not this summer. They're in Europe, a long-postponed trip. I think Mom wanted to do something different this year."

"Well, good for them," she says, a flicker of understanding crossing her face. "It must feel a little strange, being here on your own."

"Oh, don't worry about our Lucy," Dawn says, nudging me. "She won't be lonely for long."

Mrs. Farrow laughs, patting my arm. "Ah yes, where is that handsome Jack? I haven't had the pleasure of seeing him yet this evening."

The assumption shouldn't surprise me, but it still cuts deeper than it should.

"Oh, I don't know. I haven't seen him."

Mrs. Farrow frowns but recovers with a gracious smile. "Well, we're so glad you're both here tonight."

I thank her, genuinely touched, before she's swept away by a friend tapping her shoulder, eager to introduce her to their houseguests. Dawn is caught up talking to someone I don't recognize, so I take a moment to get my bearings and scan the party. No sign of Jack. But across the terrace, framed by a flickering cluster of candles, I spot Sloane, effortlessly holding court like the party showed up just for her. She catches my eye mid-sentence and breaks into a relieved grin, gliding toward me with her arms already open.

Sloane has that kind of classic beauty that sneaks up on you: refined, a little mischievous, the sort that makes people turn their heads twice trying to figure out what exactly they're drawn to. Full mouth, sharp cheekbones, eyes the color of wet sand after the tide pulls back. Her hair, a glossy shade of honey brown, falls in loose waves that always look perfectly lived-in, like she just came from a swim and somehow her hair dried into a blowout. There's an ease to her that feels unpracticed, every glance, every laugh landing just right, but underneath it, she's always reading the room.

"Lucy, oh my God, you look insanely hot," she squeals, pulling me into a hug before stepping back, taking me in. "Seriously, you're a *vision*. I'm obsessed with this dress."

I laugh. "You can borrow it anytime. Like the old days."

"You mean the days when we used to swap outfits behind your grandmother's back and pray we didn't stain anything?"

"Exactly those days," I say, grinning. "But also, *you* look amazing and infuriatingly effortless, as always."

She waves a glossy manicured hand. "Stop, you'll make me blush. But keep going." I loop my arm through hers as she begins weaving us through the terrace crowd.

"You have to catch me up," she says, leaning in conspiratorially. "What's going on with your life? Are you dating anyone fun? How's the new studio?"

We find a quieter spot tucked beneath a swaying palm and fall into conversation like no time has passed. We trade updates, her art gallery clients, my art progress, and how quiet the Lazy Daisy feels this summer. Sloane shifts her body toward me, blocking out the rest of the party. There's something about being with her, like my mess is already halfway untangled just by landing in her orbit.

"God, I've missed this," I say, finally.

She presses her arm against mine and lifts her glass in a soft toast. "We'll always find our way back."

I catch myself smiling at my glass when movement across the terrace pulls my focus. It's subtle, just a few heads turning, a couple women straightening or flicking their hair.

Jack strides in over the tiled floor, nodding to a few guys as he passes, wearing a crisp white button-down and that irresistible smile, the one that always made my stomach somersault. With a bottle of wine tucked under his arm, he greets Mr. Farrow with the kind of hug that says, *everyone here knows me, and they like me*. And they do. They always have.

Sloane follows my gaze and doesn't bother hiding her sigh. "Well, well, well. Would you look at him."

I raise my glass to take another sip, half-shielding myself behind it. "He's late."

"Interesting that you noticed," she murmurs, tilting her head. "He's also somehow...even hotter? And very much alone. Want to disappear? Want *me* to disappear? Just tell me what to do."

"No," I say, hurriedly. "We're friends. It's good."

"Mmhmm," she nods slowly, unconvincingly, but mercifully without commentary.

Jack's eyes land on mine and linger there. His smile spreads like moonlight slipping through a window.

"Didn't even have to look," he says, stopping in front of us and leaning in to kiss Sloane on the cheek. "Just followed the gravitational pull."

Sloane swats his shoulder lovingly. "You still clean up nice, Jack."

"Just trying to keep up around here," he says, turning to me as his voice lowers. "Hi, Luce."

"Hey," I smile nonchalantly. "Nice of you to join us."

He shrugs, a glint of mischief lighting up his eyes. "I timed it just right. Knew you'd be here by now."

Sloane watches us with a sharp look that could cut glass. After a beat, she sighs. "Some things never change."

Jack and I turn back toward her, and she gives a breezy little shrug. "I'm going to mingle and see about a cute boy. Or two."

She winks at me before slipping into the crowd, leaving behind the faint scent of expensive perfume. I look over at Jack, expecting him to crack a joke. But he doesn't. His gaze trails down my body before meeting my eyes again.

"You look beautiful, Luce."

I can't stop my cheeks from flushing, but I tilt my head and reply, "You're just now realizing?"

He laughs. "I just thought I'd say it out loud." He reaches out a hand, almost as if he wants to touch my hair, but then pulls back. "Your hair is already lighter than the day you got here. It's amazing how quickly it does that."

"You always say that."

Jack steps a little closer, shifting to stand beside me rather than facing me.

"These parties haven't changed too much," I offer.

"Nope," Jack replies, glancing over the room. "Same band, same tuna tartare, and I'm pretty sure that's Mr. Dunning with his third fiancée in five years."

My eyes drift to a woman in a low-cut dress laughing too loudly on the arm of someone else's husband.

I feel Jack glance over before he nudges me gently. "I know that face. You're already writing a whole narrative."

"Old habits," I smirk.

"Feels like we never left."

"We did, though," I say, meeting his eyes for a moment before turning back to the crowd. "And then we fell apart," I whisper.

I feel the heat of his gaze. "You think I wanted that?"

I hesitate, the words already pressing at the back of my throat. The late flights, the missed weekends, the slow unraveling of something that once felt sacred. "You didn't exactly stop it."

I turn and meet Jack's eyes, filled with hurt and longing. "Do you really believe I didn't want to figure it out, Luce?" His voice is quiet, careful. "You were the only thing I ever got right."

Except you didn't. I look away before he can say more, pretending to study the crowd. "I wonder if the band is taking requests."

He smiles faintly but it doesn't reach his eyes. We stand in silence for a few moments.

"I should go find Dawn," I say lightly.

Jack nods. "I think I saw her on the lawn."

I take a step away, then pause, "Good to see you, Jack."

He smiles, but it's halfhearted. "You too, Luce."

I slip back into the current of the party, determined to shake the heated look in Jack's eyes out of my mind. Why did I have to go there tonight? What did I expect him to say?

The music has shifted into something younger now, the kind of song that makes people sway in place while they pretend they're not watching each other. I spot a few familiar faces near the back patio, some old friends from surf camp, that one woman I only ever see at this party but still greet like we share a rich history.

The night becomes a soft blur of excited hugs and catching up with longtime island friends. I chat with Davis and Annie near the vintage rum tasting table. They got engaged on the island over New Year's on Davis's boat and are planning a wedding next spring at The Other Side.

I spend a few minutes with the Lennox twins, whom I used to babysit, who tell me about their semester abroad in Spain, which sounds like it consisted of tapas and sangria and very little school. They try to talk me into camping on Man Island with them in two weeks.

"Everyone's going," Lila exclaims, tugging on my arm. "We're doing the whole thing, tents, bonfire, sunrise plunge, campfire breakfast."

"You should come," her brother Finn adds. "You can be, like, the cool older girl who won't forget the sunscreen."

I laugh, holding up my hands. "I'm flattered, but I make exactly one major concession to nature per season, and it already happened a few days ago when I found a bird's nest in my outdoor shower."

They groan in protest, but I'm already backing away. "I'll send snacks though, I promise."

As I move back into the crowd, I can't help but smile, because there is something sweet about being asked. But there's absolutely no chance I'll be camping on Man Island. The last time I went was nearly five years ago, and I shared a sleeping bag with Jack and woke up with a hermit crab in my hair. I've earned my exit badge.

The band has changed to a DJ now playing a hip-hop remix of "Forever Young." I spot Dawn in the middle of the dance floor, surrounded by our friends, already barefoot and flushed. There's glitter on someone's shoulders, and at least one person is using a palm leaf as a fan.

I move without thinking. My body remembers this exact dance floor from all the previous versions of this party. I love nights like this. Underlit, over poured, completely untethered from reality. I always forget how good it feels until I'm in it. Time disappears as the music folds around us, the night stretching wide and endless.

Someone grabs my hand, warm and sure, and before I can register who it is, I'm being spun out and then pulled back in. Jack's grinning, looser than before and so handsome in the string-lit glow, like he's done this exact move a hundred times and knows exactly when to hit the beat. Because he has.

"You looked like you needed a better dance partner," he whispers in my ear.

I laugh, off balance but happy. "Is that what this is?"

"This is me saving you from Finn's elbows."

I glance over my shoulder. Finn is indeed flailing like an inflatable tube man, completely oblivious to everyone around him. "Fair point."

The songs blend one into the next, and we stay. It's hot, our skin slick from sweat, and we're grinning like idiots who forgot they ever broke each other's hearts. He keeps his hand at the small of my back, guiding me through the crowd like he never stopped knowing how.

He starts singing along to "Something Just Like This," a song we used to play on repeat driving around the island in his golf cart, and I can't help joining in. It's stupid and perfect and entirely a bad idea for me to have this much nostalgic fun with him.

"You remember all the words," I laugh.

"You made me memorize it."

"Yeah," I grin, scrunching my nose at him. You're still offbeat."

"You never minded," he says, leaning in close.

Jack's hand settles lightly at my waist, fingers applying pressure that sends chills down my spine. We fall into step like no time has passed. When the song ends, he doesn't move away. Just stands there, looking down at me like he's remembering every version of us.

Chapter Nine

THE AIR IS ALREADY THICK WITH HUMIDITY, AND THE SUN IS bright enough to make me wince as I step out of the shade of my porch and pass through the front gate. My head is a gentle drumbeat of regret, but I force myself into a slow jog.

The island is quiet in that perfect late-morning way, a faint breeze shaking salt off the palms. I wave to a neighbor clipping overgrown bushes and another walking their dog. I tell myself I'll jog into town, maybe circle around to get two miles in, then reward myself with a donut from Arthur's. A completely fair trade. But first, I want to stop by the art gallery.

The air conditioning hits like a small miracle when I finally enter, the bell jingling as I close the door behind me. The gallery smells earthy, like canvas and wood and paint. Helen is standing behind the counter, flipping through a stack of unframed watercolors. She looks up with a wave as I slip past a display of vintage Bahamas prints.

"Well," she says, setting the pages aside and studying me. "You look exactly how I felt after the Farrow party last year."

I groan. "Ugh. Is it that obvious?"

"Only to someone who's been there," she teases, walking around the long counter to greet me. "You're brave to be out running in this heat."

"I'm running on black coffee and the promise of fried dough."

Helen laughs. "Sounds like you've got your priorities straight."

I lean lightly against the counter, taking in the cool calm of the gallery, the collection of framed Amos Ferguson paintings glowing under soft spotlights. Helen watches me for a beat, something thoughtful stirring behind her eyes.

"You know, I'm glad you stopped by. I'm curating a group show here at the gallery this August, artists who really capture the essence of island life."

I smile. "That sounds amazing."

"I've been following your work online," she adds. "Your pieces have a depth that's compelling."

"Oh?" I say, genuinely touched. "Thank you."

"I was hoping you'd be in it," she says like it's obvious.

My brain stutters for a second. "Wait, really? You want to include me?"

Helen tilts her head, amused. "Of course. Why do you sound surprised?"

"I don't know." I laugh, suddenly hyper-aware of my sweat-soaked running clothes and frizzy ponytail. "Because I'm standing in your gallery looking like I just survived a tropical boot camp?"

She grins. "You could show up in seaweed and I'd still want your work in the show. You've got a voice, Lucy. A point of view. That's what matters."

Her words land heavier than she probably means them to. I've finally been painting again, for the first time in weeks, and the colors actually feel like mine. But I don't trust it yet. Inspiration's a slippery thing. I keep expecting it to disappear the moment I admit it's back. Maybe Helen sees something steadier in me than I do.

"Okay," I say, my throat tightening. "I'd love to be included."

She gives a victorious clap and motions for me to follow her toward the back room, where a long table is scattered with artist portfolios, color swatches, and a half-finished iced tea sweating on a coaster.

"I'm glad to hear it," she says, flipping open a folder. "There'll be five, maybe six artists, any more than that and it'll get crowded. Two are locals, one does those beautiful layered encaustic pieces, and the rest are visitors. I want contrast. Texture. A sense of place. And your work gives me that."

We chat for a few more minutes about logistics, tentative dates, and framing deadlines before I say goodbye and step back into the wave of humidity.

I jog back onto the path, the air still thick, the same salt wind brushing my shoulders. But I feel different. Not just excited, but lighter, like I put down a weight I hadn't realized I was carrying. I've had shows before, back in Charleston, but those always felt like something I *had* to prove, like I was trying to earn a seat that might not be mine. This feels quieter. Surer. Like being seen for something I didn't even have to explain.

After I round the corner by the Piggly Wiggly, the sun hits me again at full force. I'm tempted to skip the donut and run straight into the ocean when I spot him as he steps out the door of Arthur's. Noah.

I straighten my posture and quickly smooth my hairline. He's holding an iced coffee in one hand, talking to someone who looks vaguely familiar. His hair's still damp, from either a morning swim or maybe a shower, and he's wearing sunglasses and a vintage tee that's faded just right. He looks like he's on a movie set.

The moment that Noah spots me, he lifts his iced coffee in a wave before saying something and giving a parting fist bump to the guy he was with before turning toward me.

"Hey, Briland," he says. "Running toward me or just a happy coincidence?"

I laugh, slowing to a walk. "Let's call it fate and blame the humidity."

His smile widens. "If this is what humidity brings in, I'm a fan."

I come to a stop in front of him, the two of us hovering beside the white pineapple fence, the scent of buttery baked goods drifting outside.

"How far'd you make it?" he asks.

"A few sweaty blocks," I say. "But the donut detour was calling."

"That's still farther than I planned to get today…I was actually going to text you this morning," he says, sounding a little shy. "My friends are heading out tomorrow. We're doing dinner tonight at OVC. You should come."

A flash of Jack's face, his hand in mine, spinning me across the dance floor, flickers through my mind, but I bat it away. "Are you sure I wouldn't be crashing their last night?"

He shakes his head. "They all love you."

My cheeks warm before I can stop them. "Then sure. I'd love to."

Noah starts to back away, still watching me, that crooked smile playing at the corners of his mouth. "Perfect. I'll come by to grab you before."

He turns, walking off down the street, and I stand there a moment longer, grinning like an idiot.

I'M JUST FINISHING MY HAIR WHEN I HEAR THE KNOCK. I TWIST the last strand into place and clip it up, sweeping it off my neck. The breeze at dinner will be warm, and I don't want to spend the night battling frizz.

One last glance in the mirror. The light-yellow linen mini dress fits like it was made for me. It barely passes the sitting test, but it's worth it. The straps are delicate, one dotted with four wooden bead accents that catch the light.

When I open the door, Noah's standing there, one hand in his pocket, the other holding a bottle of wine. His green eyes move over me for a beat, maybe two, and his lips press into a soft smile.

"Too much?" I ask.

He blinks like he's snapping out of something. "No. You…" He clears his throat. "You look beautiful." The way he says it makes my stomach flutter.

"Thank you," I say, my voice a little softer than I intended. "You look nice, too."

And he does. He's wearing a well-fitted light blue button-down, sleeves rolled, and tan pants. There's something about the way he holds himself that makes the world around him blur.

"OVC's just a ten-minute beach walk if you're up for it?" I ask, slipping my phone into my purse.

"Oh yeah, that sounds nice." He kisses my cheek as he steps inside.

"Same bottle you had at White Cottage. I figured it passed the test," he says as he sets the bottle on the entry table.

"It did. But just so you know, you don't need to bribe your way in." I smile, grabbing my sandals and leading him through the house and out the back door. The breeze brushes the back of my neck, making me glad I pulled my hair up.

The sand is still warm and packed beneath our feet, the sky above us soft velvet, a few stars already visible. The kind of night that feels stolen from a dream.

"You always dress like this for dinner?" Noah asks, a smile pulling at his mouth.

"Only when I like my company," I reply, grinning.

"Oh," he says, mock-surprised. "So you *do* like me."

I bump his arm and wink. "I meant Kate."

I slow my pace and tilt my head up. "Look," I say, pointing. "The Big Dipper."

He follows my finger and studies the sky. "I used to work at a planetarium," he says.

I turn to him, surprised. "Wait, seriously?"

"Yeah. Sound design. I spent a whole summer trying to figure out what space *sounds* like."

"That's so cool," I say, awed. "So…what does it sound like?"

He grins as he puts his hands in his pockets. "Mostly layered synths, deep reverb, and a few eerie wind effects. My proudest track was a piece I called 'Saturn's Breath.'"

I laugh. "That is so specific."

"The assignment was 'make people feel wonder.' I overshot it and probably gave them minor existential dread."

"I'd pay to hear that."

He nudges me gently with his shoulder. "Careful. I might still have the files."

We walk in comfortable silence. Without a word, Noah reaches for my hand. He doesn't look over. Doesn't acknowledge it. Just threads his fingers through mine like we've always held hands on moonlit beaches.

Dinner unfolds in a haze of stories, laughter, and too many shared plates passed around. Not once do I feel like an outsider. Noah's friends are warm in that unforced, genuine way that makes you forget you haven't known them forever. Which is a relief after my hesitation over joining their last dinner.

We're tucked beneath a clear tent on the patio, the waves crashing just beyond the edge, the lanterns strung overhead casting a soft amber glow across the table. It catches on wine glasses, on the hoops in Kate's ears, and in Noah's hair every time he leans closer.

And he does lean closer. Often. I'm seated between Kate and Noah, but it's Noah I'm acutely aware of. The way his knee keeps brushing mine beneath the table, like we're on the same frequency. The way his fingers graze my hand mid-story, tracing lazy, absentminded circles on my palm.

The server continuously tops off my wine glass without asking, and I don't stop him. The buzz is pleasant and fizzy, and I'm warm all over.

Every so often, Noah's hand settles on my knee, light, far too fleeting. It's maddening in a *I might catch fire if this keeps up, or worse, if it stops* kind of way.

Kate nudges me at one point, her gaze flicking to Noah's hand and back to my face. I nearly choke on my drink. She just giggles and turns back to Miguel, not saying a word. She doesn't need to. And I'm left here, skin buzzing, undone by the quietest touch.

By the time dessert arrives, one last candlelit moment for Kate's birthday, everyone sings a little too loudly and off key. The sky overhead sparkles. I glance at Noah, who's watching me with that unreadable smile again, the one that makes my heart stutter just enough to remind me, *oh yeah, this night does* not *have to be over yet.*

After goodbyes, we step off the patio and into the hush of the beach, the dark stretching out around us. I turn toward him, swaying slightly.

"I just realized something," I announce dramatically, arms raised.

Noah arches his brow, amused. "Oh?"

I point at him, steadying myself. "You wrote my go-to running song, yet I've never serenaded you with it."

Before he can reply, I belt out a verse off-key and too loud.

He groans, tilting his head back. "Oh no."

"Oh yes," I declare, launching into a mash-up medley with maybe half the lyrics correct, the rest improvised.

Noah stands frozen, equal parts horrified and amused. "This is brutal," he says, but his goofy smile betrays him. "You're destroying the bridge."

"I'm improving it," I counter, spinning as I hit another dramatic note.

"Oh, wow," he says, steadying my hips gently. "That's an interesting take."

I give an exaggerated wink. "You're welcome."

He bursts out laughing.

I pause, out of breath and smiling. "You're enjoying this."

"You're gloriously unhinged."

"Thank you," I say, giving a little bow.

We fall into step, strolling barefoot along the shoreline, the tide rushing beside us. I start humming again, unbothered and at ease. Noah doesn't stop me. Instead, he joins in on the parts I skip, matching my melody and nudging me when I fumble.

I tilt my head. "You're not secretly laughing at me, are you?"

He shakes his head. "Not even a little."

His gaze drifts across my face like he's memorizing me. Then with a tenderness that sets my pulse beating faster, he says, "In fact, I don't think I've ever liked that song as much as I do right now."

We slow to a stop, the rhythm of our steps lost to the hush of the ocean. A few stars overhead waver in the dark, but I only see Noah, close enough that my heartbeat echoes in my chest.

He takes both my hands, strong and steady. I feel an electric certainty. He steps closer, free hand brushing a loose strand of hair from my temple. His fingertips softly graze across my jaw.

A laugh catches in my throat, nervous, hopeful. His thumb rests gently on my cheek, a quiet punctuation to every moment that led here. I lift my gaze toward his lips, and in that quiet, breathless beat, he leans in.

The kiss is slow and sure, setting my pulse racing. When I pull back, he rests his forehead against mine. Then he whispers my name and brushes his lips against mine again softly. I don't dare move. Our bodies are pressed together and his hand is tracing my arm and it's so hypnotic that I could just melt right here.

When we pull apart, I'm dizzy with the quiet pull of this new gravity between us. And he just watches me, steady, like he wants the moment to last, too.

"That was…" I start, but the words tangle in my throat.

I slap a hand over my mouth, stunned, and then I laugh. It spills out, breathless and tipsy, the kind of laugh that sounds like disbelief and giddiness all at once.

Noah watches me, smiling like he's not sure whether to be concerned or charmed.

"What are you laughing at?" he asks.

"I don't know," I gasp, which only makes it worse.

He catches me in his arms, laughing now, too, as he pulls me close.

"Okay, let's get you home," he murmurs against my temple, voice rough around the edges. Another kiss follows, this one featherlight on my forehead.

When we reach my back door, the porch light casts a soft pool of gold around us. Noah doesn't let go of my hand right away.

He studies me for a beat, head tilted, mouth tugged into a smile with a gaze I'm finding harder and harder to resist. "Alright," he says, a hint of regret in his voice. "This is where I say goodnight."

Wait. Goodnight?

"You don't want to come in?" I ask, trying to sound casual and failing completely.

His smile shifts, same curve but new depth. Something laced with heat. One hand rises, fingers grazing the beads on my dress strap, then traces up the side of my neck.

"I've already imagined what happens if I stay," he says quietly. "That's exactly why I can't."

My breath catches. "Oh," I say, stupidly. "Okay."

His thumb drifts along my jaw. His eyes are darker than I've ever seen them. Tension crackles in the air between us, sparking hotter because it doesn't ignite.

"You have no idea how much I want to," he says. "But not tonight."

And then he kisses me. Slow at first. Deliberate. Then faster, hungrier, like he's sealing it in. Like he's making sure I remember. My fingers curl into his shirt and pull him into me without thinking. I don't want him to stop.

But he does. He pulls away and his fingers linger against my wrist.

"Good night, Briland," he murmurs. Then he turns, hands in his pockets, and walks into the warm dark like he hasn't just undone me.

Twenty minutes later, I'm still floating. I was so dazed in the shower, I stood there for a full minute trying to remember if I'd already conditioned my hair. I did it again just to be sure. Possibly a third time. My hair has never been silkier.

Now, tucked into bed, damp hair in a towel, my phone chimes on the nightstand. I reach for it and forget how to breathe. It's a photo from dinner. A candid. I'm mid-laugh, leaning against Noah, my whole body angled toward him. But it's his expression that unravels me. He's looking at me like I'm his favorite song.

Before I can even process the soft detonation in my chest, another text lights up the screen.

Unknown Number: Girl, he is so smitten.

A beat later:

Unknown Number: This is Kate btw.

A squeak escapes me as I drop the phone against my chest, grinning like a lunatic. My cheeks are on fire, my heart a loud drumbeat in my ears. I stare at the photo until I fall asleep.

Chapter Ten

I WAKE UP TO ANOTHER POUNDING HEADACHE AND AN OVER-whelming sense of embarrassment. For a few blissful seconds I just lay here, warm and cozy in my sheets, replaying last night. The way Noah looked at me over dinner, the lingering beach walk, the way he touched my face, the way he kissed me like he never wanted to stop.

And then. *Oh. My. God.* The singing. I groan, rolling onto my stomach and burying my face in my pillow. I serenaded Noah. With one of his own songs. I peek one eye open at my phone on the nightstand.

> **Noah:** Hi Songbird
> **Noah:** Call me when you get up and moving

My bed seems to tilt under me as I stare at the message. My thumbs hover over the keyboard. I could reply with a joke. A flirty line. Something unaffected. But the flashback of last night makes me pause. I sang to him. Badly. And he walked me home but didn't come inside. Said he'd *imagined* what would happen if he did.

I drop the phone back onto my comforter and toss off the covers. I need a distraction.

The air is already thick with humidity as I stroll into town, earbuds in, someone else's love problems distracting me from my own. The morning sun bounces off the glossy porches of storefronts that have been caked with multiple layers of paint over the decades. I push open the glass-paneled wooden door of Briland Bloom and the scent of white tea and sandalwood candles washes over me, mingling with the soft notes of a French café playlist playing overhead.

Dawn is behind the counter straightening a display of silk scarves. Her braids are piled high in a loose, glorious halo that looks both effortless and intentional. She's wearing a cotton tank dress the color of papaya and hoop earrings that sway when she moves.

When she looks up and sees my hungover face, she plants her hands on her hips. "What is happening? And stop letting out all my air conditioning."

"I don't even know," I answer with an exasperated sigh as I close the door behind me. "I went to dinner with Noah and his friends last night and had the best time. Like, maybe *too* good of a time? I serenaded him on the beach on our walk back to my house, and he definitely did *not* come inside."

Dawn takes this in and whistles. "Okay, back up. All the way to the beginning."

I join her behind the counter, folding scarves and filling her in. I start with Noah picking me up. I walk her through the whole night, the dinner, the banter, the beach walk, the singing. By the end, I'm even more mortified than when I walked in.

Dawn places both hands on my shoulders and tilts her head down to stare directly in my eyes.

"Lucy, I'm not gonna lie. The singing? A little cringe. But also? Adorable. And the fact that he said goodnight and went home? That's a green flag, not a red one. Noah seems like a good guy. This is *not* as bad as you're making it out to be."

"You think?" I groan, tilting my head back. "I mean, logically, I hear you. But I'm still dying inside."

Dawn pats my shoulder. "You were relaxed and letting your guard down. You were...unfiltered. I love unfiltered Lucy."

She pauses, softening. "Try to feel it out when he calls."

Right. That. "I woke up to two texts from him."

Her face lights up. "What did they say?"

I pull out my phone and read them aloud. Dawn waves exasperatingly. "Lucy. For the love of God. Just call him and put yourself out of your misery."

I stare at the screen and roll my shoulders back, trying to shake off whatever's rattling under my ribs. "What if I wait till later? Like, this afternoon? Or tomorrow?"

She gives me the Dawn once over. Brutal. Effective.

I look back down at the screen. "I think I'm just gonna text him back."

"Lukewarm," she shrugs.

"It's not lukewarm," I argue, already typing. "It's chill. Which is appropriate, because I'd like to recover some shred of dignity."

I wince, typing slowly.

Me: Last night was fun! Still smiling...and
maybe regretting the concert.

Me: How are you?

"Meh," Dawn says with bored indifference as she reads over my shoulder.

My phone buzzes almost immediately.

Noah: Chocolate chip ice cream might help with the regret. Want to join me?

Dawn fans herself with a scarf. "Oh *look*, I was right. He likes you."

I smile, heart fluttering. But I already know my answer.

Me: Tempting, but I promised myself I'd actually get some painting done today. Raincheck?

His reply is quick and easy.

Noah: Anytime.

I heart the message then lock my phone before I can over-think it. Dawn reaches across the counter and gently pats my hand. "Thatta girl. Now go home, blast something good, and paint out your feelings."

Chapter Eleven

BY THE TIME THE SUN STARTS DIPPING IN THE SKY, I'VE PAINTED through my anxiety and am psyching myself up for another night out. Tonight is The Wexlers' annual full moon party. The guest list is always impossibly exclusive. Last year there were two pro-football players, one late-night talk show host, and one Oscar-level actress. No one misses a Wexler party. They own a huge chunk of land at the end of the island, and their estate is a waterfront masterpiece that stretches from beachside to bayside.

The night is famous for its spectacle: two live bands, one set up on the sand for the midnight moment when everyone gathers barefoot beneath the rising moon. At the stroke of twelve, the band begins playing "Dancing in the Moonlight," resulting in half the party jumping into the ocean in all of their finery. It's the kind of party that ends up splashed across society columns the next morning, always captioned like a secret only insiders know about.

I've known Dinah Wexler since her family bought on the island over ten years ago. To the outside world, she is the definition of a socialite—glamorous, unbothered, always a little ahead of the curve, a trait she clearly inherited from her mother. But her boldness doesn't stop at fashion or opinions. It shows up in the way she loves people—loud, unwavering, and without apology.

By the time I step onto the Wexler estate, the party is in full swing. From outside, the house is glowing, with light spilling from the floor-to-ceiling windows, illuminating the manicured lawns and towering palms swaying in the breeze. I'm relieved I chose my long, silky pale peach Johanna Ortiz dress. It skims over me perfectly but doesn't try *too* hard, and I won't have to hold it down in the breeze coming off the water. The spaghetti straps dip into a dramatically low cascading neckline, and I paired it with gold jewelry.

Music softly pulses through the air, making the whole place feel alive. And Dinah's right at the center of it all. Perched on the edge of a sleek white sofa next to the nearly Olympic-sized pool, infinitely long legs crossed, appraising the crowd like she owns the place. Which, to be fair, she kind of does. The second she spots me, her face lights up.

"Lucy! Finally." She rises effortlessly, floating over in a short, ivory, crystal-embellished dress that catches the light with every step. I recognize it from Chanel's latest collection. She sparkles like the party was thrown just to match her.

The first time I met Dinah was at a painfully dull dinner party. I remember watching her across the table—espresso brown waves falling over her shoulders, a dress far too expensive for a teenager, and that restless, gleaming energy of someone already plotting her escape. She toyed with the clasp on her

Cartier bracelet like it was a ticking clock. When she caught my eye, she smirked like we were already in on the same secret.

She leaned over her plate. "You look like someone who knows there's a better party somewhere else."

An hour later, there we were, slipping through the side gate of a beachfront wedding at the Ocean View Club.

"Confidence is key," she'd whispered, gliding straight into the reception like the velvet rope had always been on her side. Nobody questioned it. Dinah has the kind of beauty and presence that bends reality just enough to make you believe you belong, too.

We danced barefoot in the sand. We flirted with boys. We got caught once, maybe twice, but Dinah batted her lashes and spun a lie about being the groom's cousin's house guest, effortlessly smoothing it over.

By the time we wandered back down the beach, the hem of my dress was damp with salt spray, and my cheeks ached from laughing.

"I'm never crashing another party without you," Dinah had said, looping her arm through mine like we'd been best friends forever.

And now I'm lucky to call her one of my best friends. For the last decade, she's been in my corner no matter the miles between us, name dropping my art to her editor friend at *Vogue*, and more recently jumping on a flight after my Jack breakup with a martini shaker and matching silk, feather-trimmed pajamas. Dinah doesn't just show up, she upgrades the moment.

"I was about to send a search party," Dinah teases, sweeping me into a hug.

"No way," I laugh. "Like I'd miss this."

Her eyes dance. "I almost did! I forgot to book my flight, but luckily I hopped on a friend's jet this morning! Oh Lucy, I've missed you!"

Dinah snags a passing server, plucks two martinis from the tray, and hands me one. Her dark wavy hair cascades down her back, and her skin is golden, with a radiance that comes from weekly facials.

"To us. May we avoid any lurking crypto bros tonight."

Dinah scans my face. "You're flushed," she continues after a beat. "Like you have a secret."

I immediately blush, waving her off. "You've been back for five seconds and you're already in detective mode?"

She winks. "Please. I'm fresh off Portugal, dodging yacht boys with commitment issues. I live for mysteries I can actually solve."

I shake my head, but she cuts me off. "Actually, there's someone I want you to meet tonight," she says. "Tall. Charming, but not in a narcissistic way. A little broody, maybe book-ish?"

Before I can reply she declares loudly, "Oh, hi Jack."

I turn and follow her gaze. He looks maddeningly handsome and perfectly composed, dress shirt unbuttoned just enough, that damned smile playing on his lips.

"Hi Dinah, Luce," he says, coming to a stop in front of us.

Dinah arches a brow, her smile widening devilishly. "And here I was, assuming you'd forgotten all about us here on Harbour Island. How long have you been hiding, friend?"

Jack leans in for a bear hug. They've always traded barbs like currency but the affection beneath is unmistakable. "Long enough to accidentally overhear some matchmaking plans." He glances at me with a tight smile that doesn't reach his eyes. My heart does a clumsy somersault.

Dinah doesn't miss a beat. "Don't be jealous, Jack. You had your chance. *Chances.*"

Jack takes it with a smile, but there's a flicker beneath it, a sadness you'd miss if you didn't know Jack well. And I do.

Dinah watches us for a beat, and I can feel her taking the temperature of the room before lifting her glass in a toast. "Well, I need to get some of these greetings out of the way, so if anyone needs me, I'll be over there pretending to care about my dad's little shipping boats."

After Dinah walks away, Jack angles toward me and says, "Have you been painting at all?"

I exhale, grateful for the change of topic. "Yeah, a little. I'm trying to get into a groove. You'd probably laugh if you could hear me rambling while I sketch out studies."

"I could always tell when you disappeared into it," he laughs. "You'd start talking to the page instead of me. Like the sketch needed a pep talk."

Something stirs low in my chest before I can stop it. A flash of sun-warmed sand. My sketchbook balanced on my knees, the page rippling in the breeze. Jack stretched out beside me on the beach, one arm bent behind his head, watching me instead of the water. I remember the way he inched closer every few minutes, pretending not to. The quiet heat of his thigh against mine. His fingers brushing my ankle as if by accident, lingering just long enough to make it impossible to concentrate on the lines in front of me.

A server appears offering a tray of miniature conch fritters. Jack shifts, taking an easy step back, the space between us reappearing and somehow accentuating how close we were just seconds ago.

I glance around the room and spot my friend Thomas with a guy I don't recognize near the bar, pulling off his signature open-shirt look like he's still a teenager. He catches my eye, gives me a wink and a wave, equal parts affection and mischief.

Thomas has always been the glue, the instigator, the unofficial cruise director of our group. Seeing him here, laughing with someone new, makes the years collapse in on themselves.

Lazy Daisy, late afternoon. We'd spent the day helping Gran clean up the yard for one of her parties. Thomas dragged speakers out to the porch. Allie and I strung lanterns through the palms, and Jack quietly tackled Gran's list of to-dos, including fixing the beach gate latch that she refused to replace. By the time the sun went down, we'd all ended up around a small beach bonfire. Blanket piles and rum punch. Thomas was playing a guitar terribly but with dramatic flair. Allie and I tossed popcorn into the fire just to hear it crack, and Jack stood at the edge of it all, shadowed in firelight, coaxing Thomas into one more chorus.

I can't remember exactly what Jack said to me that night, something teasing, but I remember how it made me feel. Giddy. Helpless and hopeful. We weren't together then, but God I wanted to be.

Thomas's laughter carries across the room and I smile. "God, he hasn't changed."

"Not one bit," Jack says.

"Gran always loved Thomas's stories about his love life. She said it was better than any soap opera."

Jack laughs. "She loved when he'd come over."

"Hey, you know that rickety gate latch you used to fix for her?"

He turns to me with a smirk. "The one she wouldn't let me replace because 'you don't throw something away when you can fix it?'"

"That's the one. Well, it's broken again."

An older man interrupts, clapping Jack's shoulder and pulling him away. Jack gives me an apologetic smile, the kind that almost says *stay*, before turning toward the man.

Another server glides past balancing a tray of caviar-topped tater tots with a dollop of crème fraîche. The Wexlers always travel with their chef, a woman who can make the best grilled cheese of your life as well as a seven-course meal, and this time I can't resist. I snag one without hesitation as Helen materializes at my side, tugging my elbow with the kind of loaded grin that means she's about to drop a bomb.

"Lucy, I knew I'd see you here, or I would've called. I got the most unbelievable call today. From Graham Vale." She pauses for effect, and I widen my eyes, mirroring her expression. "He's offered to host the art show. At his home!"

It takes a second for the words to register, like my brain doesn't quite understand them. "Graham Vale, the photographer? The coffee table book Graham Vale?" I ask, stunned. "But no one's seen him here in years."

"The very one," Helen nods, practically vibrating. "I nearly dropped the phone. He said he wanted to do something for the art community. When we went over the artists, he mentioned knowing your work."

I'm so stunned I hardly know how to form words. Graham Vale has seen my paintings. They'll be in Graham Vale's house, the place everyone whispers about but no one has ever been to. In the last twenty years, anyway. It sits back from the road, hidden behind clipped hedges and a large gate that remains locked. I can't imagine my canvases hanging on those walls.

"Why now?" I finally ask. "He's been practically invisible for over a decade."

Helen leans in, lowering her voice. "I don't know. But that's exactly why it's exciting. He's been so quiet that the press will have a field day with this. Graham Vale opening his gates again in such a public way? It'll be in every art publication you can think of. Which means," she squeezes my arm, "so will your work."

A nervous laugh bubbles up. "I can't believe it."

"I have a hunch it's more than just timing. People don't come out of hiding for no reason."

Her words prickle against my skin though I can't say why.

Helen straightens, her voice bright again. "This isn't just an island event anymore, Lucy. This is going to be *the* story." She gives me one last gleeful look before melting back into the crowd.

I stand there for a moment, trying to slow the thrum in my chest. Graham Vale. Hosting us. Hosting *me*. And beneath all the excitement, a strange flicker of something I can't quite place, like maybe this isn't random at all.

In a daze I begin to wander through the crowd until I spot Dawn and Sloane sitting by the pool's edge. I head over and sit down, the stone cool beneath me, my dress pooling around my legs. Sloane moves her clutch to the other side to make more space.

"Sitting on the ground in the middle of a party never looked so good," I sigh.

"Oh," Sloane says, perking up as she pulls a slim velvet pouch from her clutch. "I almost forgot!"

"Oh my God, tell me you didn't bring your Tarot cards?"

"I didn't bring my Tarot cards," she deadpans as she fans them out with a flourish. "I'm still learning, but I'm pretty good at single-card readings. Shall we?"

Dawn leans forward with a serious look. "Well, since you already have them here, let's see what the universe has to say tonight."

Sloane grins as she holds out the deck. Dawn hovers her hand above the cards for a beat, eyes narrowed in concentration.

"Okay, be nice to me." She draws a card and lays it down with a flourish.

"The Chariot," Sloane says, voice dropping to a whisper. "Success, determination. Taking Control."

Dawn's eyes go wide. "I'll take that."

Sloane smiles. "You're capable of navigating challenges and asserting your power. Never forget it, Dawny."

"You're such a boss," I add.

Sloane reshuffles the cards and fans them out in front of me. I hesitate, brushing my fingers on the deck. I draw a card and place it on the stone between us. Sloane flips it.

"The Two of Cups."

Dawn leans in, eyes darting between us. "That's love, right?"

"Usually," Sloane nods, her tone dipping into something reverent. "A deep bond, emotional harmony. Soulmate energy."

The word feels like a wound. *Soulmate.* For a second, the laughter from across the pool fades, and my eyes zero in on Jack across the party. And somehow he's staring at me like he knows exactly what I'm thinking. *We were soulmates. Why wasn't that enough? Why wasn't I enough?*

Dawn nudges me, breaking the spell. I shake my head and come back to the moment.

Sloane steadies the air with her voice. "It's also about love and balance within ourselves."

Something about this feels true. I feel like I'm coming back to myself on this island. Learning to trust myself and my instincts.

"I must admit, being here with you guys back in our favorite place is the balance I've been missing. You're pretty good at this, Sloane," I say, placing my card back in her deck.

We all look up as Dinah glides over, barefoot now, her sparkly dress catching the light just so. Sand clings to her ankles and there's that unreadable smile, like she has a secret she hasn't revealed.

"I knew I was missing the best part of the party," she moans, sliding gracefully onto the stone beside us. "And here you all are, having your full moon goddess moment without me."

Sloane grins, shuffling the cards. "Perfect timing, Dinah."

Dinah eyes the deck. As Sloane begins to fan the cards, she draws her card without hesitation and turns it over.

"Knight of Cups," Sloane reads, her voice lilting with interest.

Dinah's brow lifts skeptically. "A drunk knight?"

"It's the romantic. The dreamer. Someone chasing something, or someone, with their whole heart."

I lean in. "So like, an emotional quest?"

"Exactly," Sloane nods. "It's about following your feelings, letting inspiration lead the way, even if it's messy or a little risky." She tilts her head, assessing Dinah. "It also means emotional intelligence. The ability to be graceful and diplomatic."

"Well, Dinah has that in spades," Dawn quips.

Dinah purses her lips, considering. "If only I could find a guy actually *worth* whole-heartedly pursuing," she says dryly, but there's a flicker of something in her expression.

Her gaze drifts out over the water, and then she nudges me gently with her shoulder. "Hey, I've been meaning to steal you for a minute. Come meet someone."

I raise an eyebrow. "Who?"

She smiles, eyes dancing. "The guy I told you about. You'll see."

I glance at Sloane and Dawn, who are both trying not to laugh. I rise, smoothing my dress. We move through the crowd, Dinah just ahead of me, her bare feet silent on the stone path, the curves of her dress shimmering with each step. She doesn't say where we're going, just gives me one of those looks over her shoulder, all glinting eyes and knowing smile.

"He's around here somewhere."

Before I can respond, someone calls her name. She pauses mid-step as a tall guy steps into view, wearing a linen blazer and embroidered Stubbs & Wootton loafers.

Dinah turns to me briefly. "Give me one second."

I nod, watching her float into a practiced greeting, kissing both his cheeks, laughing at something he whispers. She's a master of this world, polished, poised, and completely in her element. I hang back, quietly observing. I don't recognize him, but he has unmistakable energy, the kind of presence that makes everyone around him pay attention.

"Sorry," she says in a lowered voice, turning back toward me. "Had to say hello. That's Felix Devereux. His family owns, like, half the hotels in Europe."

I glance back at him, and he's talking to someone else but still watching Dinah. "Whoa."

She grimaces. "I'm exaggerating, but it's a lot. Also, he's the worst. He's arrogant and a total playboy. And he and Dix had some sort of run-in this past winter. I didn't really get the details. I don't know what he's doing on Harbour Island, but I didn't want to ask and keep the conversation going any longer than necessary."

"Speaking of grace and diplomacy," I laugh. "I never would have known you felt that way, watching the two of you. How is your brother, anyway?"

"Oh, you know Dix, never slowing down. But he's good. He won't be here this summer at all though, a positively unforgivable offense in my mother's eyes, made worse by the fact that my father is somehow to blame."

"What happened?"

"Oh, some work situation that Daddy signed off on and now deeply regrets," she laughs.

We keep walking, her dress brushing mine as she steers me past the dance floor and down a quieter lush garden path lit with tiny white lights.

"Anyway," she says, squeezing my arm conspiratorially, "back to the mission."

We round a hedge wall and step onto a smaller terrace tucked into the side of the estate. And there's Noah. He's leaning against the stone railing, deep in conversation with someone I don't recognize. But the second he sees me, his smile widens and he adjusts his posture.

"Hi Briland," he says with an unmistakable glint in his eyes, like he's not surprised to see me.

Beside me, Dinah lights up like she just successfully engineered a royal engagement.

"You two already know each other?!" she asks gleefully.

Noah doesn't look away. His gaze deepens. "We've met."

"Well then," Dinah says breezily, already stepping back, "I'll leave you to it. I'm going to rescue my mother from doing the 'Say So' dance. Pray for me."

I turn back to Noah, trying to keep my expression calm even as I fidget, twisting my rings, smoothing my dress.

"I didn't know you'd be here."

"Neither did I. I met Dinah during lunch today. She knows a friend of mine and extended an invitation."

"Well, I'm glad she did."

He leans back on the rail, arms loose, relaxed. "I didn't plan on staying long," he says. "But something told me you might be here."

My fingers go to my hair, tucking a strand behind my ear, the same spot his hand brushed last night. His gaze dips there for half a second, pupils dilating.

"I've had your singing stuck in my head all day."

I groan, rolling my head back. "God. Don't remind me. I regret everything."

"I don't." His voice is low. "I've thought about it more than I should."

My breath stalls. The words hang between us, soft and weighted. He sees the way I react and steps closer.

"I meant what I said before I left," he adds, voice rougher now.

I swallow. "Which part?"

His eyes don't move from mine. "The part where I said I wanted to stay."

For a split second, I imagine what staying would have meant. And then Jack is there, too, not in the memory, but in the consequence of it.

"Noah, hey man, come jam with us!" A guy with unruly hair waves from near the stage.

Noah groans, a cringing smile curving his lips. "That's Leo," he says. "I wrote with him once. He never quite takes no for an answer."

I laugh. "So…run?"

He glances back at Leo and then at me, warmth in his eyes. "Tempting," he says, "but I've been seen."

I gesture at the stage. "Please. I'm dying to see this side of you."

He pauses, flustered in a way I haven't seen before. "Alright," he says. "But only because you asked politely."

He squeezes my hand then moves to the stage where they hand him a guitar. He sits, and after a short discussion begins playing. The music flows through his fingers like it knows the way, even if this isn't one of his songs. A woman's voice drifts in over the notes, melting into the hum of the party. Noah leans into it, completely absorbed. Watching him, the party feels softer, more intimate.

They shift to something slower. Noah's posture is relaxed, talking gently to the band between songs. He's utterly at ease, like that guitar was made for him.

"He seems to know what he's doing," Jack says softly beside me.

I turn and look up. Surprised to see Jack standing there with a thoughtful expression, the gold flecks in his eyes sparkling in the glow of the party light.

"He does," I say carefully.

He nods, then tips his chin toward the stage. "Think he takes requests?"

I roll my eyes playfully. "He probably shouldn't from you. Have something in mind?"

"Of course. Something for old times' sake."

"Like what?"

"Whatever gets you to roll your eyes at me again."

And I can't help it. I do.

"There it is," he says with a real smile this time, the kind that hits low and warm. For a second, neither of us says anything. The music fades into the hum of conversation, and I feel it, the pull of so many moments caught between us.

His gaze flicks to my mouth, just once, before he clears his throat. "It's probably time to drag my dad out of the cigar room before mom finds him."

"A time-honored tradition," I laugh a little breathlessly. "Good luck. Say hi for me."

He waves, an emotion flickering and gone before I can analyze it.

I stay a couple songs longer, watching Noah in silhouette. He's still on stage, laughing with the band, completely absorbed, like the rest of the world's fallen away.

He glances up just as I start to turn. Our eyes meet, barely a second, just long enough for me to lift a hand in a small wave. His smile flickers, slow and easy, before he looks back to the strings.

The music shifts as I make my way through the yard, louder now, someone tuning a guitar down on the sand for the midnight beach set. Some guests are starting to drift that way in clusters, bare feet and silk catching the light. I could join them, or stay and see where the night with Noah might go, but something about that conversation with Jack, those old feelings and memories, has left me off balance. I can still hear my grandmother's voice in my head, that soft scolding about not throwing away what still works if you're willing to care for it.

I step off the Wexlers' back terrace and down toward the beach to walk home.

The heat in Noah's eyes. Jack's unreadable smile. It's all too much to sort through at this hour. I don't want to pick sides or follow threads or untangle what's pulling at me tonight. I just want the sand under my feet, the hush of the waves, and the quiet permission to let it all wait until morning.

Chapter Twelve

THE LINE AT SWEET SPOT SNAKES OUT ONTO BAY STREET, A SLOW parade of sunburned tourists, golf carts, and locals waiting for recovery smoothies and green juices. The place smells like ginger, mango, and espresso all at once. Inside, the lime green paint feels like vacation, and Allie waves from a corner booth, two green smoothies and a banana monkey bowl waiting for me.

"Hi, Sleeping Beauty," she greets as I slide onto the bench.

"Is it that obvious I just rolled out of bed?"

She laughs and nudges the bowl closer. "Years of experience. I'm just jealous of your flexibility. I've been up since five."

"Oof," I say, accepting the smoothie. "I owe you. Did you have fun last night?"

"Dear God, yes. I danced with my husband for the first time in months—in heels no less. It was basically a second honeymoon," she says, eyes shining.

I smile, leaning back in the booth. "You were radiant."

She fans herself. "I needed an excuse. Honestly, I'm kind of itching to dive back into the world."

I raise an eyebrow. "Back to work?"

She nods, thoughtful. "Yeah. I miss the routine. Is that weird?"

"Not at all," I say. "You're allowed to want what you want."

My phone buzzes. I look down.

> **Jack:** Call me when you have a sec? Nothing
> big, just a question.

Allie's eyes narrow. "You're doing that thing with your shoulders."

I force a smile and show her my screen.

She shrugs. "Jack hates typing. If it's more than three words, he calls."

I look back at the screen, frowning. "But with a caveat and a promise that it's 'nothing big?'"

She softens. "True. If he's leading like that, it could be something."

Silence lingers. Then she adds, "He probably just didn't want to call this early."

I glance at the clock. "It's 9:20. Maybe he thought I was still asleep?"

"Maybe," she murmurs, leaning closer. "You and Jack have been circling each other forever. Maybe it's time."

I stir the straw in my smoothie. "Time for what?"

"All in, or…," she pauses, eyes steady, "…moving on."

My heart beats a little faster. "I thought we settled that two years ago. Magical summer, summer ends. He returns to New York. I head home to Charleston. We fall apart."

I catch her gaze, flickering with something unspoken. I know this is hard for her, too, stuck between her friend and her brother.

I release a breath. "Okay. I'll call him."

An hour later, I'm back home, idly doodling in Milly's notebook while I wait for her to come by to talk through a few house things, when I decide to just get it over with and call Jack.

"Hey," I say, keeping my tone easy as he picks up.

"Hey, Luce." His voice is warm, though there's something tentative tucked around the edges. "What are you up to?"

"I'm just waiting on Milly. She's coming over to talk house stuff."

"Dangerous combo," he says lightly. "You two could level the place if you start making your lists."

I laugh, pacing slow laps between the island and the counter. "I'll try to restrain myself. I had breakfast with your sister this morning."

"Yeah, she mentioned that," he says, and I can practically hear the grin through the phone. "Said you went to Sweet Spot." There's a pause, then I hear a door close quietly on his end. "Actually, I wanted to ask you something."

I stop pacing.

"Some clients of mine are here from New York. We're grabbing drinks tonight. Would you want to come?"

"No pressure," he adds quickly. "I just…thought you might like them, especially Chloe."

His voice is careful. Hopeful, in that quiet Jack way that lands somewhere between awkward and adorable. Part of me wants to keep my distance. Say no. Remind myself I'm not his girlfriend anymore.

Instead. "Sure."

Twenty minutes later Milly steps inside with her favorite straw hat and a folder tucked under her arm. "You've been busy," she says, nodding toward the sketches spread across the table.

"I have a big day of painting ahead of me," I say. "What's on today's house list?"

"The usual suspects." She flips open the folder. "The roof still needs patching. Jay should be coming this week. And we should probably deal with the loose tile on the back steps. Oh, and the vines around the arbor are threatening to take over again." Milly scans her notes. "Anything you've noticed?"

"Just the beach gate latch," I say, reaching for my water. "It's jammed again, won't close all the way."

Milly frowns. "Really? It was fine this morning when I went down to the beach."

"Huh. Maybe it's just temperamental."

She shrugs, already moving on to the next item. "Like everything else on this island."

After she leaves, curiosity gets the better of me. I wander down the sandy path to the beach gate, expecting to still find it hanging by a thread. But when I test the latch, it clicks shut, easy and sure. At closer inspection, I see fresh oil gleaming faintly on the hinge.

Jack. Of course he did. I rest my hand on the wood, smiling despite myself.

At exactly 6:30, I hear the soft thump of his footsteps outside. My breath catches as Jack steps into view on my porch, hair damp and slightly curled, wearing a soft pink linen shirt. I try to shake away the thoughts of how good he looks as I step out into the warm air, but his chiseled jawline and broad shoulders are impossible to ignore.

He smiles, deep brown eyes flicking away from the curve of my shoulder where my dress drapes.

"You look beautiful," he says easily, like it's the most natural thing in the world.

"Thanks," I grin, lifting my chin. "You look freshly showered."

His laugh is low. "That'll go straight to my head."

"You'll never believe it," I say with raised eyebrows, "but the beach gate is magically fixed."

Jack runs his hand through his hair, eyes dropping away. "It was a quick fix."

"I owe you one," I say, meeting his eyes for longer than necessary.

The warm breeze lifts the hem of my green silk dress, and it dances across my upper thighs as he gestures for me to lead. Bougainville brushes my elbow as I pass through the front gate.

On our way through town, he tells me about the couple we're meeting. His voice is relaxed but there's excitement underneath it. "They're nice. I've been working with them for a couple years. Chloe's an author, mystery novels I think," he says, glancing over at me.

We stop for a flock of roosters loudly crowing and crossing the road.

"You *think* she writes mysteries?" I tilt toward him, leaning into the question.

"Okay I know she does, but I haven't read any of them," he replies, eyes forward.

"Why does that not surprise me, Jack?" I tease, leaning my left elbow on the back of the seat between us as I turn toward him. "You still don't read fiction?"

He leans toward me, that cheeky smile daring me to argue. "Numbers are more my thing, Luce."

I flick his shoulder. "That's not very well-rounded of you."

He laughs. "I promise you this, if you pick up a finance book, I'll read one of Chloe's."

I shake my head, still smiling. "I'm not falling for that."

"Falling for what?"

"You're trying to trap me into tax talk."

He laughs as he parks in front of Rock House. The boutique hotel sits high above the bay, its white-trimmed shutters glowing in the late evening light. Inside, the terrace restaurant hums softly with low conversation and clinking glassware, part old-school supper club, part island hideaway.

We find a secluded lounge nook, a loveseat and a pair of striped rattan chairs angled toward the sea. The breeze stirs the warm air scented with garlic, citrus, and something faintly floral from the garden below. Beyond the balustrade, the harbor flickers with moored sailboats and the faint music drifting up from Dunmore Town. It feels private here, a pocket of calm above the noise.

"So," Jack says unhurriedly as he sits beside me on the loveseat. "How's your new series coming?"

"Good, it's finally starting to come together," I say, aware of how close we're sitting.

He nods confidently. "I knew it would. I want to see it."

"You'd be surprised. I'm painting seascapes. I was never really drawn to them before, but now, I don't know, it feels like exactly what I'm supposed to paint."

"Does it help you feel connected to your grandmother?" he asks.

I pause, the idea hitting unexpectedly. "Maybe. I hadn't thought of it like that."

Of course he'd frame it that way. Jack has always had a knack for seeing straight through me, for naming the thing I'm circling before I'm ready to say it out loud. It's dangerous how easily he still does it.

"Helen at the art gallery asked me to be a part of the summer show," I say, my cheeks warming. "It's going to be at Graham Vale's estate."

He looks up, his hand finding mine without thinking. "August, right? I wouldn't miss it."

I glance down at our hands, then back up at him, clearly caught off guard. He notices, too, his fingers loosening as he pulls back, something flickering across his face.

He grimaces slightly, like my surprise hurts him. "I stopped into the gallery a couple days ago and Helen mentioned it," he explains.

"Aw, summer Jack," I joke, elbowing him lightly in his side. "Has time for midday art gallery perusals and beach walks."

He's quiet, looking out toward the harbor. "It's nice being here, you know? Slow pace, fresh air, roosters as my alarm clock."

"You mean you haven't missed the honking cabs?"

He lets out a breath that could almost be a laugh. "Definitely not."

A flash of emotion clouds his eyes, and it's clear there's more he's not saying. I open my mouth to ask, but at the last second pivot to a safer topic like the coward I am, launching into a story about Milly's recent DIY mishap.

I'm leaning forward, giggling at Jack's impression of his dad trying to figure out their internet when a well-dressed couple appears at the edge of our circle.

Jack stands immediately, flashing a grin as he pulls the man into a friendly handshake and leans in to air-kiss the woman's cheeks.

"Lucy, this is Chloe and Charles," he says, placing a light hand on the small of my back as I rise. "And this is Lucy."

Charles shakes my hand and says, "Looks like we weren't the only ones who decided to come early."

Jack smirks. "Great minds think alike."

I glance over at Jack as their exchange clicks. *He brought me early on purpose.* I don't say anything, but a corner of my mouth lifts.

Jack gestures for Chloe to take the loveseat beside me, while he and Charles drop into the club chairs across from us. Jack was right. I instantly adore Chloe. She's funny, sharp, and effortlessly charismatic. The kind of woman who talks with her whole body and makes you feel like you've known her forever.

"Wait a second," I say, pausing mid-story as recognition hits. "I've read some of your books! There was one I read a couple of years ago that I couldn't stop talking about!"

Chloe claps her hands together. "Really! Which one?"

"The one about the missing elementary teacher. I devoured it on a trip to Miami."

Her face lights up as she leans closer. "Stop, I love that! Okay, be honest, when did you figure out the twist?"

"Not until embarrassingly late," I admit.

She gives my hand a squeeze. "Excellent. I can't stand when someone tells me they saw it coming on page five. Like, 'no you didn't, Cindy.'"

We laugh, and I glance over and meet Jack's gratified gaze with wide eyes. "Wait a minute. You know I love Chloe's books!"

Jack laughs, mischief in his eyes. "I can neither confirm nor deny." Despite how much I'm trying to move on, this is the man I've always loved —kind, playful, adoring. How do I move on from this?

I clear my throat. "Jack mentioned y'all have kids?" I ask, needing to change the subject before I'm overwhelmed.

"A boy and a girl," Charles confirms. "This is our first trip away without them in a while, just the two of us."

"And we are thriving," Chloe adds, eyes twinkling. "I love my babies, but I hadn't eaten a hot breakfast that I didn't cook in months."

"Cheers to that," I say, clinking her glass.

"We're staying at The Dunmore," she tells me. "It's been amazing. We've got one more night after this, and I don't want to leave," she glances back at her husband with a wistful smile.

"Lucky you," I say, sipping my Sky Juice, my favorite Bahamian cocktail made with fresh coconut water and gin. "I love The Dunmore."

"It's always been her favorite." Jack's staring at me as he says it.

Chloe glances between us, a gleam in her eye. We order a round of appetizers to share, spicy shrimp, the daily crudo, and salty plantain chips warm from the fryer. The conversation flows easily, and at some point, Chloe tugs me toward the makeshift dance floor in front of the band.

"We're dancing," she announces as she pulls me in, and soon we're spinning as the band plays a Caribbean song I don't recognize but instantly love. Jack and Charles hang back, watching us with matching amused expressions as they chat about stocks and accounts, I'm guessing.

"You're both lame!" Chloe calls out.

Jack raises a hand in surrender. "Someone's gotta hold the table."

"Excuses," she mouths, but ten minutes later we successfully drag them up to join us.

By the time we collapse back in our seats I'm a sweaty, happy mess.

"This is the best night," Chloe declares, fanning herself with her napkin. "I don't want it to end."

"Then let's not yet," Charles says, leaning back against the cushion of his chair and glancing at Jack and me. "Another drink somewhere?"

Jack turns toward me, waiting but not pressuring.

And I could. I could keep going and stretch the night a little further. It's tempting. But I know myself. And this moment already feels whole, and more than I expected.

"I need to tap out while I'm ahead," I say, smiling apologetically at Chloe. "But you guys go. The night is young and you're on vacation."

She leans in, angling her phone toward me and showing me my Instagram account. "Okay, but before you escape, is this you?"

I laugh, nodding as I follow her back.

"Good," she says, satisfied. "I'm keeping you."

Jack's eyes twinkle proudly beside me. "Everyone keeps Lucy."

I study his face, entirely too relaxed, and I wonder if he meant to say that out loud. Jack and I walk back toward his golf cart in an easy silence. He's carrying leftovers, a half a slice of key lime pie Chloe insisted we take. When we reach the cart, he walks me around to the passenger side. Jack hasn't even made it to the driver's side before a heavy raindrop hits my shoulder, followed by a fierce boom of thunder.

Jack glances up just as a raindrop hits him on the forehead. "Uh oh."

One breath later the sky cracks open, dumping warm rain in heavy sheets. Within seconds we're drenched. My green silk dress clings to me, molding to my skin. Beside me, Jack's linen shirt goes sheer, the muscles of his back visible beneath it. His hair drips, curls loosening.

"Oh my God!" I yelp, pushing my wet hair off my face. "This came out of nowhere!"

Jack's shoulders shake as he laughs, water collecting on his eyelashes. He lifts one hand from the wheel to swipe it away, useless.

"You want me to pull over?" he shouts over the rain.

His voice is warm, teasing, like he knows I'm actually thrilled to be caught in a storm.

As Jack turns left at the corner by Coral House, he pulls us to a stop against the pink stucco wall, the golf cart tucked beneath the heavy spill of bougainvillea. It muffles the rain, like someone lowered the volume on the night. Steam rises from the pavement around us, and for a second, neither of us says anything. Our hair drips, our shoulders rise and fall, and the night smells like salt and wet flowers.

Jack catches me watching him, breath uneven from laughter.

"You okay?" he asks quietly.

I nod. "Just…drenched."

His gaze drops, briefly, to where my dress clings. Heat sparks up my spine.

Jack glances sideways, lips parted like he's about to say something.

"What?" I ask, breathless, too aware of how close our knees are.

He shakes his head, but the look lingers. "Nothing. Just… I love being with you. Even in a golf cart in a thunderstorm."

My stomach flips. Warm, dangerous.

Jack clears his throat, fingers tapping once against the wheel like he's remembering what he's supposed to be doing. "Alright," he says, "let's try this again, shall we?"

He nudges the golf cart forward, tires splashing through shallow puddles. The bougainvillea canopy falls away and the rain rises to full volume again, warm and relentless. Thunder rolls, low and close.

We don't talk at first. The kind of silence that is full of everything neither of us managed to say back there. Water drums against the plastic roof. Streetlights blur through the rain, turning the pastel houses into watercolor.

Jack brakes gently at a tight turn, and our knees brush once then settle against each other, warm through the soaked fabric. Jack goes very, very still.

"You cold?" he asks, eyes still on the road.

"A little," I admit.

He exhales through his nose, quiet, and reaches across the small space between us. His fingers find my wrist, circling it lightly, his thumb brushing the thin stretch of skin there.

"You have goosebumps," he murmurs. My pulse leaps against his thumb. His eyes flick down as if he felt it, then back to the road, jaw tightening just a little. He doesn't let go.

Rain continues to drum against the roof in steady sheets. The world outside blurs, but all I can feel is the steady spread of heat where his hand holds mine. He gives the slightest squeeze, barely there, and I think, for a breath, he might say something he can't take back. Instead, he guides us around the corner into my drive, knuckles white on the wheel.

Jack rolls us to a stop in front of Lazy Daisy, the windows glowing warm against the storm. The rain hits harder here, drumming on the roof like applause.

Jack finally looks at me, and something in his expression softens. "You looked really happy tonight, Luce," he says. "I love seeing you like that."

Warmth spills beneath my ribs.

"And, I mean…" He gestures vaguely at my soaked hair and clinging dress, a tiny curve to his mouth. "Even drenched in a thunderstorm, you're still the most beautiful girl I've ever seen."

My breath catches. His hand is still loosely around mine, thumb unconsciously brushing once before he catches himself. He goes still. The rain drums around us.

Jack's voice dips. "I missed talking to you like this. Like we did tonight."

The admission is small, but it means more than any compliment.

I lean in without thinking, just an inch. He does too. My knees slide between his thighs, and my free hand curves around his neck. His other hand grips my thigh, and the air between us thickens. His eyes flick down to my lips and back up to meet my gaze.

"Lucy," he says, barely a whisper. "Tell me to stop."

I don't.

We hover there, foreheads touching, breath mingling, close enough to feel the shape of a kiss. My heart trips over itself. His hand tightens slightly around mine, not pulling. *Steadying me.*

Lightning flashes and I jump, breaking the moment. I exhale and lift my forehead from his with a soft shake of my head.

"I should go in."

He swallows, jaw flexing once as he nods.

"Yeah," he says gently. "Go warm up."

He lets go of my hand slowly, and the absence aches.

"You want to come in and borrow a towel?" I ask, helplessly wringing out the end of my dress.

"I'm okay," he says. "I've been through worse for a good night."

I smile, shaking my head as I climb out. Water squishes loudly between my toes as I run toward the porch. When I reach the covered steps, I glance back.

Jack's still sitting there in the rain, elbow hooked over the wheel, watching me as if it isn't pouring sheets all around him. He looks so good it hurts, and for a second I consider running back to him. To a kiss I know will be all-consuming.

"Night, Luce," he calls. The heat in his eyes is palpable even from here.

My voice barely makes it past the lump in my throat. "Night."

After a long, hot shower, I'm sitting on the end of my bed in pajamas when my phone buzzes.

> **Jack:** Tonight reminded me of that Junkanoo night a few summers ago. Those ridiculous squeaky sandals of yours, and that thunderstorm. Still one of my favorite nights.

A grin tugs at my lips before I even realize I've started typing.

> **Me:** That was the best night, wasn't it?

And then a couple of beats later a scene tugs at my memory.

Me: You forgot about having to give me your shirt because mine became completely see-through.
Jack: No I didn't.

A long pause, then:

Jack: You looked really great in that shirt.

I stare at the screen.

Me: Which one?

There's a long pause.

Jack: Both.

My pulse is everywhere. Before I can stop it, my mind goes straight back. To Jack standing behind me, hands warm and steady as he tugged my shirt over my head, the night air cool against my skin. The way he pressed his mouth to my shoulder like he was trying to memorize me. Like he had all the time in the world and none at all.

I think of Jack's hands at my hips, the familiar weight of him, the way he always slowed things down right when I wanted to rush. His mouth at my throat, my name said like a promise.

I start typing something reckless, backspace, start again. He beats me to it.

Jack: Get some sleep, okay?
Jack: Good night, Luce.

There's care in those words. And restraint. But I still feel the want.

Me: Night, Jack.

I set my phone down before I can admit anything else.

Chapter Thirteen

I SHOULD BE PAINTING. TECHNICALLY, I *AM* PAINTING. THERE'S A canvas in front of me, a mix of blushy pinks already layered across the surface, the start of another shoreline study. This whole collection is supposed to feel like Harbour Island: soft mornings, salt-stiff breezes, that impossible blue the water turns an hour before sunset. It's the first time I've ever tried to bottle a place I know so well.

And maybe that's why it's gotten slippery. Every time I dip into a color, my mind ricochets somewhere else.

Looming pressure doesn't help. The show will hang at Graham Vale's house. The legendary Graham Vale, who somehow knows my work. Where editors, collectors, and everyone on this island with deep pockets will drift through the rooms with strong opinions, loudly shared. People collect photographs of this island because they want to own a piece of it. I'm trying to paint mine because I want to feel closer to Gran, the legacy she left behind, the brushstrokes I can't ask her about anymore.

I'm set up on my back patio wearing a bikini, trying to catch a little sun. The breeze carries in the scent of sunscreen and a whiff of grilled pineapple from somewhere down the beach. It's distracting in the best way. Harbour Island is like that. You might come here with plans, and then the island laughs and hands you a Goombay Smash instead.

I'm running out of time, too. Sloane, Dinah, and Thomas are coming over at six for Mahjong. That gives me an hour. Which technically means I *could* get another layer down on this painting, if only I'd stop wondering whether the familiar grilled pineapple scent is coming from the house two doors down and start moving the brush in my hand.

Noah called this morning and invited me out on the boat with his friends in a couple of days. A barbecue on Sand Dollar Beach. And then there's the rainstorm with Jack. It's been nearly a week but my brain hasn't stopped replaying that night. What almost happened. What I wanted to happen. But maybe it doesn't matter, because I haven't heard from Jack since.

I sigh and dip my brush again, this time pulling in a sharper line of indigo across the water. A little contrast. A little clarity. I tell myself I'll stay out here twenty more minutes, then shower and slice some limes.

I HAVE THE DOORS THROWN OPEN, AND THE WAVES MINGLE WITH the Coldplay mix coming from the speaker. I've mixed a batch of coconut margaritas with pineapple garnishes, a bowl of my legendary French onion dip, which is really just a packet mixed with sour cream, and Sloane's favorite kettle chips, dressed up in a stoneware dish.

Thomas arrives first, all but two shirt buttons undone, a large bowl in hand.

"So you *did* make the guacamole," I exclaim in greeting, accepting the dish like it's the gift from the gods that it is.

"I told you I would," he admonishes me.

Sloane and Dinah show up together a few minutes later as Thomas and I set up the tiles. Sloane's sun-kissed brown bob skims her shoulders, accentuating her collar bones. Dinah's long dark hair is wrapped up in a high bun, showcasing a caftan that looks casual but I know probably costs as much as a vacation.

"Okay," Sloane leans forward as she begins dealing, eyes glittering. "I have sip sip. Did you hear who was at lunch at The Dunmore today?"

I smile at Sloane's use of the Bahamian phrase for gossip as Thomas theatrically chimes in, "Please say someone famous. I'm starved for a celeb sighting."

Sloane grins. "Oh, he's famous. *Very* famous. A certain British singer with phenomenal fashion sense who Dinah's mildly obsessed with."

She can only be talking about one person. My head whips toward Sloane as Dinah gasps and nearly jumps out of her chair. "You're lying!"

"I swear on my new Missoni bikini," Sloane says, holding up a hand. "He walked in with two guys and a girl, low key, sunglasses, oversized hat, but it was *him*. He chatted with an older couple while waiting for his table and told the server to bring them a round on his tab."

"No," I whisper. "That's so charming. He's not allowed to be so cute and talented *and* charming."

"Apparently he ordered grilled lobster and a Pellegrino," Sloane says. "And then he tipped like two hundred dollars."

Thomas whistles low. "Honestly, I'd marry him for that alone."

"Same," Dinah mutters, leaning back dramatically. "The moral of the story is never skip The Dunmore."

We all nod solemnly. Harbour Island's magic isn't just the pink sand and colorful historic cottages. It comes in many forms, one being that your celeb crush could casually show up at lunch.

Thomas claps once. "Shall we?"

As we play, I am very clearly not paying attention. I discard tiles without looking, repeatedly forget it's my turn, and nearly knock my drink over twice.

Dinah eventually levels me with a loving but exasperated glare. "Out with it. Now. Before I pelt you with Mahjong tiles."

Sloane hums thoughtfully. "I give her two minutes before she cracks."

"I give her thirty seconds," Thomas says, not even looking up from arranging his tiles.

I hold my hands up in defeat. "Fine. Noah invited me to a beach BBQ on Sand Dollar Beach."

Everyone stares at me, clearly underwhelmed.

"That's it?" Thomas asks. "That's the big distraction?"

Dinah narrows her eyes. "Was it like a sexy invite or a 'bring a side dish' invite?"

"It was…a cute invite," I admit.

Sloane shrugs. "Okay. Not nothing, but not panic-inducing, Lucy."

I chew my lip. "…And a week ago, Jack and I almost kissed on the way home from drinks."

Thomas lets out a strangled noise and dramatically faints out of his chair, one hand clutching his chest. "Tell my mother I died doing what I loved. Gossiping."

Dinah's eyes narrow. "Back up. Drinks?"

"At Rock House," I say. "With his clients. He brought me along because he knew I loved the wife's books. So he sort of surprised me."

Sloane smiles slowly. "Jack surprised you with drinks with one of *your favorite authors?*"

I nod. "He said he thought I'd want to meet her."

Thomas presses a hand to his chest. "Oh honey."

"And then you almost kissed," Dinah says carefully.

"In a rainstorm," I add. "Like a full, cinematic rainstorm. It was really hot."

Dinah and Sloane exchange a loaded look that makes my stomach flip.

"And it was really confusing," I finish. "And we haven't spoken since."

Sloane's eyes soften. "Of course you're confused."

"I don't know how to feel about any of it," I admit. "Noah feels easy. Jack feels…like Jack."

Thomas pats my hand. "Ah yes. The most dangerous feeling of all."

Dinah points at me, and I brace myself. "You don't have to know," she says firmly. "And you haven't made anyone any promises."

She pauses, making sure I'm listening. "But you do need to make one promise to yourself. Don't be scared of what your future could look like. Whether it's with someone new…"

Sloane picks up seamlessly, "…or with someone we all know is still very much in love with you."

I cover my face with my hands. "You think he is?"

Thomas snorts. "Lucy, he's been over here fixing things around your house and telling the entire island about your art show. That man is down bad."

I laugh despite myself, something in my chest loosening picturing Jack telling people about my art.

Dinah reaches across the table and squeezes my hand. "You're allowed to be messy. But just make sure you're honest with yourself."

Thomas raises his coconut margarita. "To being messy."

We clink glasses. And Dinah's right. I've made no promises. Not to Noah. Not to Jack. Just to myself.

Chapter Fourteen

WE ARE *NOT* GOING TO NEED A BIGGER BOAT.

It's not flashy, just really nice. It's a sleek center console, the kind that cuts through chop without rattling your teeth. It's a soft Bahama blue, the decks sun-bleached white, long bench seats along the sides, and there's a shaded T-top overhead casting cool relief from the sun.

Noah stands barefoot near the helm, looking adorable in his backwards cap pulled low over his hair, and one hand wrapped around a water bottle. There's a basket of clean striped towels tucked beside a built-in cooler packed with lime-spiked sparkling water and local Kalik beers.

He smiles when he sees me. "Hey Briland."

"Nashville," I reply, taking his offered hand and stepping aboard carefully in my mini wrap skirt.

There are six other people onboard, including a couple music industry people I'm beginning to recognize. I clock Jacob right away, gold chain glinting against his collarbone.

He looks like a pop star. Noah said that the album they've been writing together is one of his favorites yet.

Up front, wide cushioned loungers are scattered with navy throw pillows, and a small teak table sits on polished hardware between them, already set with a plate of cut mango and chips. A speaker tucked discreetly near the console plays reggae with just enough bass to feel like it belongs on the water.

I settle near the back, legs tucked beneath me, sunglasses on, content to observe, as the boat cuts cleanly through the water, skimming past sprawling vacation homes with private docks.

Jacob is mid-story, something about a chaotic music video shoot in Mexico involving a broken drone and a goat that refused to leave the frame. I don't catch every word. What I notice instead is Noah laughing beside me, low and unguarded, his shoulder pressed against mine. Every time we hit a wave, our hips bump, close enough that I can feel it echo through me.

"You good?" he says under his breath, turning toward me ever slightly.

"Yeah," I say with a light smile. "I'm just soaking it in." His arm drapes lightly over my shoulders.

His thumb grazes my arm once, absentmindedly. A few minutes pass like that before someone shares a container of pineapple soaked in what tastes like rosé. It's delicious, and I have to stop myself from grabbing a fourth piece.

When we anchor off Sand Dollar Beach, the pineapple is long gone and a couple of the guys are getting the grill set up on the beach. Noah tugs me to the back conspiratorially before he and I drop into the water together and let ourselves drift a little way from the boat. The water is impossibly clear, the kind that turns your skin into a shimmer. I lean back and let it hold me, toes barely kicking, hair fanning out around my shoulders as the voices behind us grow smaller.

"So," Noah says, turning to face me more fully. "Tell me, how's Bahamas Lucy different from Charleston Lucy?"

I tilt my head, "What makes you think they're different?"

He shrugs, still floating. "You here versus somewhere else. Nothing changes?"

I think about it. "Hmmm…I drink rum at lunch. I go on boats with strangers. I leave my phone in the bottom of the beach bag for hours without checking it."

He smiles. "That explains the text delays."

"I sometimes forget I own shoes and regularly make my outfit choices based on my tan lines."

"I like your tan lines," he says as he draws a finger lightly along my shoulder, making me shiver.

"What about you?" I ask, dipping the back of my head in the water. "What makes Bahamas Noah different from Nashville Noah?"

He floats a little closer, enough that I feel the current his kicks make underwater.

"I sleep," he sighs. "Like, actually sleep for longer than five hours. And I wake up without a hundred notifications, or if I do, I don't worry about them like I do back home. I get in the water at least twice a day. I write things that I don't show anyone."

I file that last part away.

"I also," Noah adds, "swim with pretty girls who say things like 'I'm just soaking it in,' when really she's calculating the exact vibe of everyone on the boat."

I laugh. "I wasn't calculating. I was…observing."

"Exactly." He floats even closer now. "I think Bahamas Lucy's dangerous."

"Little old me?" I ask, amused, raising my sunglasses and fluttering my eyelashes at him.

He nods slowly. "Yup, little old you."

A slow thrum coils in my stomach. We're drifting together now, his hand brushing mine, and neither of us pulls back.

"You forgot to mention that Bahamas Lucy is also an excellent kisser."

My breath catches. "And Charleston Lucy isn't?"

He smiles. "I wouldn't know. I only know this one."

I watch him for one heartbeat. Two. And then I lean in and kiss him. Pushing away any thought of Jack, because I've made no promises. Noah meets me halfway, unhurried. His hand slides to my waist beneath the water, pulling me toward him, his fingers warm and slippery. His lips are sun-warmed and citrus sweet, but it's the faint scrape of his scruff that sends chills down my spine.

When we join the others on the beach, the lobster is crackling over the small grill, and Jacob is melting butter in an aluminum foil vessel over the grill grates.

Noah's pulled into a conversation with one of the guys with a camera slung around his neck, so I drift over to the low picnic table where two girls are cutting watermelon. The one wearing a white crochet bikini looks up and smiles as I grab a drink.

"I love your necklace," she says. "Is it Hart?"

"It is," I say, automatically reaching for the gold charms.

She nods approvingly. "Very cute, I love her line."

"How do you know Hart?"

"My ex used to live in Charleston," she says, wrinkling her nose. "Dated him for two years, broke up with him on the sidewalk while waiting for a table at 167 Raw. Very public. Very good decision."

"That's very specific," I laugh. "I live downtown, just a few blocks from there."

She leans back, taking me in. "I could totally see that. Charleston girls have a look, in a good way," she assures me. "I miss the shopping there. I used to spend hours on King Street in all the boutiques."

"My art studio is really close," I say, grinning. "I spend more time on King than I should."

Our conversation segues into a discussion about Charleston real estate prices, winding through favorite brunch spots and Bravo gossip. Everyone has a take on the *Southern Charm* cast. The conversation is easy even though we're just meeting today.

Everyone's quieter in that mellow, sun-dazed way once we're back on the boat. I settle into the back corner cushion again, my damp hair twisted into a knot at the base of my neck. Noah sinks down beside me without a word, one arm slung behind me, fingers grazing my faintly sunburned shoulder.

I can still feel that kiss between us, soft and electric, hanging there like it's waiting to happen again.

"New mix," Jacob announces as he taps at his phone and nods at the speaker.

A soft guitar trickles out, the kind of stripped-down melody that doesn't ask for my attention so much as claim it. Jacob's voice comes first, rich and smoky. Then another joins, and my breath catches before I can stop it. Noah. He doesn't look at me, just sits there, legs stretched long, gaze fixed on the horizon like it's any other song on any other afternoon.

The lyrics are simple at first, circling the weight of a glance, the way someone walks into a space and doesn't leave it the same. The tension, the not quite knowing but aching to, pulled through the melody like a thread. *She moves like I've heard this song before but forgot the words.*

Goosebumps prickle along my arms. I shift, stealing a glance at Noah. He's still gazing out over the water, but his hand drifts against the bench, thumb brushing the bare skin at my hip. Around us, the boat speeds forward, cutting through the turquoise water, the wind tangling my hair.

The final chord fades, swallowed by the sound of waves against the hull. Jacob looks back. "Still rough, but it's getting there."

"It's beautiful," I say, my voice smaller than I intend.

Noah finally looks over, and his cheeks are the faintest pink. "I didn't know he was going to play that," he murmurs, almost embarrassed.

"I'm glad he did," I reply, and the words feel loaded.

When we dock, everyone's gathering their things, and Noah's helping Jacob clean up the boat and gather his stuff while I hover near the edge of the dock, stalling.

I could just say goodbye. I could let this day be enough. But I don't want it to be over yet. Not with Noah. And even though Jack's smile pops into my head, I push the vision aside and cross the dock slowly, pretending to adjust the strap of my bag. Noah glances up as I reach the boat.

"Hey," I say, "What are you doing later?"

"Not sure. I'd like to run home for a shower. You?"

I nod and clear my throat. "Do you want to come over?"

His brows lift, just a little.

I keep going before I lose my nerve. "After your shower… if you want."

For a second, time seems to stall as I fumble, before his face breaks out in a beaming smile. "Yeah. That sounds good. Give me like, 45 minutes?"

The heat in my chest spreads just a little. "Okay," I say, suddenly shy. "So, I'll see you in a bit."

As I turn to walk away, I can feel him watching me, and for once, I'm glad I didn't try to play it cool.

I can't decide what to wear. Everything feels either too boring or too obvious. I dig out a pair of soft cotton shorts and a fitted grey tank top. Hopefully I look like I didn't try at all, even though I've changed outfits three times.

I light a candle in the kitchen. And another one in the living room. Then I overthink it and blow out the second one. But now the room smells like a blown-out candle. It's not giving casual.

Was I being impulsive inviting him over? No, that's not fair. The way I felt floating next to Noah, the way he sang those words, that didn't feel like nothing. There is chemistry here. I lean my head back and think about our kiss. The way his lips moved over mine. The way he touched me like he'd wanted to for days but was letting me lead. The way his hand slid beneath the water, fingers finding the curve of my waist like it was already his favorite place.

I almost don't hear the knock. When I open it, he's there, freshly shaved, a clean navy T-shirt clinging to his shoulders.

"Hi," I say.

I hear him say hello, but all I can see is the way his chest rises and falls against his shirt.

"Come in," I say, stepping back to disguise my blush.

He walks through the door, and the house feels instantly smaller.

"I lit too many candles and then panicked," I blurt out as he looks around. "That's why it smells like I'm hosting a séance."

He laughs, following me into the living room and dropping onto the edge of the couch. I settle beside him, close but not quite touching.

He looks at me and grins. "Is this the part where you pull out a Ouija board?"

I snort. "If only I had one."

"Sorry, bad joke. I might be a little nervous," he says, grinning.

"Why are you nervous?"

He shrugs softly. "You're kind of intimidating."

That makes me laugh again, harder this time. "Me? I lit a candle and second-guessed my outfit five times."

"Yeah? That makes me feel better," he smiles and slowly runs his eyes over me. "I like this, by the way."

I hop up from the couch, jittery. "Do you want something to drink? Water? Wine? I think there may be a beer or two that a friend left behind."

He follows me into the kitchen and leans against the counter as I open the fridge.

"Or I could make you a cocktail?" I ask again.

"Are you trying to ply me with alcohol?"

"I'm trying to stay busy so I don't combust," I say over my shoulder.

"Noted," he says. "But just for the record, combusting with you wouldn't be the worst way to go."

I give him a look as I jump up to sit on the island, my legs swinging slightly as I get settled. "Are you always this smooth, Noah?"

"No," he laughs. "I'm usually much smoother."

He moves over to stand in front of me. "Like I said, you intimidate me. And I like you."

His eyes flick down to where my knees are brushing his shorts and then dart back up to hold my gaze. He slowly places his hands on the island beside me, just enough to frame me without closing in. My breath catches, but I don't move.

"Can I kiss you again," he asks, voice rumbling, "or are we still debating my delivery?"

I swallow, heat spreading up my neck. "I think we've covered it."

He watches me as he steps closer. I can feel the change before anything happens, the heat between us, the shift in the air, the part of me that knows exactly what's coming next and doesn't want to rush it.

"Lucy," he says, voice low, a slight question in his tone.

I tilt my chin up, the quietest yes. "Noah."

He leans in slowly, painstakingly stretching the tension until it aches. I lean forward to meet him, just barely, until our lips skim. Not kissing. Not quite.

We hover like that, this soft, fluttering, almost kiss. I gently press my forehead to his as I draw in a shaky inhale. The wooden countertop is cool beneath my legs while every other part of me is on fire. Noah's hands slide to the backs of my thighs as he steps forward into me, and I wrap my legs tightly around him.

Then the kiss grows deep and hungry. His fingers dig into my thighs as I melt into him. He easily lifts me off the counter without breaking our kiss, my fingers winding up the back of his neck and into his hair as he carries me through the house like he already knows where the bedroom is.

And he definitely does now.

Chapter Fifteen

SUNLIGHT KNIFES THROUGH THE SHUTTERS AND LANDS DIRECTLY across my face as the crows from the annoying rooster who has taken residence in my backyard screams. I groan and roll over.

The room smells faintly like candle wax and Noah. For a minute, I let myself stretch into the quiet. But when I reach over, the other side of the bed is cold.

I stare at the pillow beside me, at the small crease where Noah's head was, and then push back the covers. My camisole from last night is slung over the chair, but I'm still in the shorts I changed into before he came over. Right. They never came off. My cheeks heat anyway.

I grab my phone off the nightstand.

> **Noah:** Didn't want to wake you. I have an
> early morning at the studio. Call you later?
> **Noah:** Last night was nice

Nice? It's not a bad message, but it lands with a thud. I check the time stamp. Sent two hours ago.

I slip out of bed and pad down the stairs, hair a mess, my robe barely tied.

Then I hear it: clanking. Not soft clanking but loud, obtrusive construction clanking. I pause at the front window and peer out at two men in my front yard. One of them is Jay, the contractor Milly and I have been chasing to finish the roof on the old garage.

The other one, standing with his arms crossed, nodding like he owns the place, is Jack. Wearing a sweaty grey T-shirt, navy mesh shorts, and sneakers. Probably just got back from a run.

I watch as he and Jay exchange a few more words. Jack nods, they both laugh, then Jack turns and walks down the path toward his place without looking up. No glance toward my house.

I let the curtain fall, drawing my robe tighter around me and exhaling sharply through my nose. *Seriously?* I don't need him managing my roofline like some kind of thoughtful ghost. I can't decide if I'm annoyed that he was here or that he left without saying anything.

I SPENT MOST OF YESTERDAY UPSTAIRS IN MY NEWLY SET-UP studio, bare feet on hardwood, Olivia Dean playing on repeat, painting pouring out of me like it has just been waiting for the right time. Something big and swirly and electric. It felt good. I didn't check my phone until after sunset, when I had two newly finished pieces and paint all over me. And on my porch

I found a small box of oatmeal chocolate chip cookies with a folded note tucked under the lid.

Looks like I missed you - N

There was a text, too. Sent an hour after he dropped them off.

Noah: Left something for you on the porch.
Just…hi.

I replied a quick thanks. But that's all that's transpired.

Now, as I pull up to Dawn's house, I smile as I hear the voices streaming from the backyard. It's nothing fancy, just a few girls, drinks on the deck, a long wooden table pulled out onto the lawn covered in mismatched dishes and melted candles. Dawn grilled shrimp and cherry tomato skewers. One of Dawn's shop girls brought a charcuterie board pretty enough for Instagram. I contributed the pimento cheese that Milly brought earlier today when she popped by for a visit.

Allie arrives right after me with Felix in a sling, a gold sparkly scrunchie in her top knot that makes her look more like a chic babysitter than someone who birthed a whole human. She's dancing him in small, swaying circles near the edge of the deck while chatting with Dinah, who is dressed in a cotton sundress but still looks like she just disembarked from a yacht where she broke at least one heart.

Sloane's laughing with Dawn over something I missed the beginning of. I recognize the slinky long Prada skirt she bought at a vintage shop during a trip we took to Miami a few years ago.

"It was *very* flirty," Sloane says, raising her voice for everyone to hear. "The vibes that Dinah was giving in her post last night."

Dinah barely blinks. "It was one story."

"One photo of you sitting very cozy with Armand Duval," Dawn adds, raising an eyebrow.

"We ran into each other at Coral Sands." Dinah says, tossing her hair with a flick of her wrist.

"Who is this guy?" I ask, reaching for another shrimp skewer.

Dinah grins over her water glass. "I think he can only be described as a *man*. 'Guy' feels too elementary."

"Okay, so who is this *man*?" Allie asks, gently bouncing the baby in her lap.

"Armand Duval," Dinah says. "He's a chef."

Sloane purses her lips. "Oh wait, I didn't connect it before. I know this guy."

Dinah's gaze swivels toward Sloane with an urgency she forgets to mask.

"I've met him once or twice," Sloane explains. "He's always surrounded by food and wine editors and women named Céleste."

"He's very French," Dinah rationalizes, shrugging her slender shoulder. "And very charming when he wants to be."

"Sooo…was he charming last night?" Allie asks, unable to hide her grin.

Dinah releases a slow, unbothered smile. "He bought me an extra dirty martini and told me my aura was soft gold."

We all groan at once.

"That's the most cringe thing I've ever heard," Dawn says.

"It worked anyway," Dinah winks. She sips her drink, already appearing bored of the topic and attention.

Dinah has a long history of choosing charming, rich guys who inevitably let her down in ways so cinematic they almost don't feel real. There was the Palm Beach philanthropist who flew her to a charity ball, introduced her as his "plus one," and then left with his ex-wife. The London tech founder who sent her a first-class ticket to visit him…and then canceled on her mid-flight. And the venture capital guy who insisted he "couldn't do serious" right before publicly proposing to a swimsuit model at a regatta a month later. Dinah laughs it off like it's all good gossip, but sometimes I catch the flicker in her expression, like the gossip is getting old.

Allie turns toward me, baby still sleeping soundly in his sling. "And how are *you* doing?" she asks.

I nod automatically. "Good."

"You just seem quiet tonight." She leans in, adjusting the strap of her sling, then adds quietly, "Jack mentioned he saw Noah leaving your house yesterday morning."

"He did?" My breath catches before I can steady it.

Allie nods, rocking lightly from side to side. "He…noticed."

Jack's always noticing but nowhere to be seen. "Yeah, Noah spent the night," I admit. I open my mouth to continue but am immediately cut off by Dinah.

"Excuse me. *Who* slept over?"

All the group chatter ceases as everyone turns to me. Allie gives me an apologetic grimace as Sloane sets down her glass and plants both hands on the table like she's ready for an interrogation. "You *have* been suspiciously lowkey tonight."

"I have not," I say.

"Yes, you're being evasive," Sloane says, pointing a perfectly manicured finger at me. "Which is practically an admission."

"Tell us everything," Dinah says. "Immediately."

I groan and lean back in my chair. "There was a boat. And rosé-soaked pineapple. And then Noah stayed the night."

"Was there sex?" Sloane asks, eyes gleaming.

I pause. The collective gasp is instant.

"Ohhh my God," Dawn whispers. "There *was*."

"There was not sex," I say firmly.

"Was there *almost* sex?" Dinah asks, whipping her napkin in the air.

I groan, burying my face in my hands. "You guys!"

Allie gives me another apologetic look. "Okay guys. Maybe Lucy's not ready to be grilled about this."

"Where was this consideration when we were discussing my night with Armand?" Dinah scoffs as she reaches for more wine. "Your turn, Lucy. We need the deets."

"We *did not* have sex. But, yes, he slept over, and we made out…heavily. And there may have been a song," I offer, finally.

"Wait, what kind of song?" Sloane leans in. "Like, a song *for you?*"

I pause, which is all they need.

"No," Allie whispers, eyes wide. "Did he serenade you?!"

"No, no, it wasn't really like that," I say, trying to rein it in. Dinah's jaw drops. "You are his muse."

I laugh despite myself. "It seriously wasn't at all like that. He didn't even play anything. Jacob did."

"Ohhh," Sloane nods, like that explains everything. "The friend did the thing. Classic. Who is Jacob again?"

"Jacob is the musician that Noah's here working on an album with."

"Okay, so," Dinah leans in. "Is this still like, a summer thing? Or are we talking actual feelings now?"

I wince, not ready for this deep dive. "It's not serious."

"Allie, did you say Jack *saw* him leaving? What exactly did he say?" Dinah demands.

I turn and watch Allie as she rocks Felix back and forth, clearly trying to downplay the event. *Yeah, what exactly did Jack have to say?*

Allie shrugs. "He just said it matter-of-factly and then went on the longest run of his life."

Dawn finally weighs in. "Nothing matter-of-fact about it. That man's been running on broody restraint all summer."

I shake my head, maybe a little too quickly. "I saw Jack yesterday morning. He was just standing there in my yard. Talking to Jay. And it's not the first time he's been lurking around."

"Talking to Jay about what?" Dinah asks, confused.

"I don't know. The garage roof?"

They all stare blankly at me.

"Well, there you go," Sloane says slowly. "He's managing your roof guy." She gains steam like she's delivering a closing argument. "You hooked up with Noah, Jack saw the aftermath, and he's still out here coordinating home repairs for you. So…which—"

"Nope," I say, cutting her off. "We are not playing 'Would You Rather' with my love life."

But it's too late. My eyes meet Dawn's and she gives me an empathetic grimace.

Chapter Sixteen

I HAVEN'T SEEN NOAH SINCE HE LEFT MY HOUSE. DAYS AGO. We've texted a little, mostly jokes, quick check-ins, nothing that asks for anything. He's been busy with studio stuff. I've been relieved for the time and space. But it also stings a little that he hasn't tried to see me again.

Jack jogged past my front gate yesterday. Shirtless. He glanced over, and I'm not sure if he caught me gawking from behind my window or not.

Dawn, Allie, and I have been drinking since a very late lunch at Sip Sip—Sky Juices, lobster quesadilla, ceviche, and a very deep life talk that devolved into what we'd each bring to the table in the event of a zombie apocalypse. Dawn volunteered to seduce the enemy, Allie took command of operations, and I, unhelpfully, would be in charge of vibes. Now Dawn and Allie are downstairs in my living room rallying, which is how karaoke ended up on the table. I should be going to bed. Instead, I'm putting on more mascara to go sing badly in public.

I pull on a short, light-pink cotton dress that requires minimal effort and slide pink tinted gloss over my lips. Before I can overthink it, I text Noah: You should come to karaoke.

Before we head to the bar, we make a quick detour to Allie's so she can put Felix to bed. Allie fumbles with her phone, laughing. "I think I texted Drew that we were coming, but I'm pretty sure it came out as 'girls incoming hot and hungry.'"

The door swings open before she reaches the handle.

Drew stands there, taking in the scene with a grim grin. "I thought you were exaggerating."

"I never exaggerate," Allie says sweetly, throwing her arms around his neck. "We need food."

"You smell like irresponsibility," he growls, stepping back to look at her with a gleam in his eyes.

"And yet you still married me," she says, patting his cheek and turning to go check on Felix.

Jack and Allie's mom, Janice, pops her head out of the kitchen with a cheerful, "There's wine in the fridge, girls!"

I give her a quick hug. She smells like lemon hand soap, warm and familiar, reminding me of the summer days I used to spend here happy and certain about everything.

"Hi, sweetheart," she says softly, giving my arm a gentle squeeze. "I've missed seeing you."

"Me, too," I say, and I mean it.

As she turns back toward the kitchen, something unsettles me. This night, this version of me, it doesn't match the Lucy she knew. The Lucy who used to curl up on the couch with Jack eating popcorn and watching movies.

A clatter of a pan pulls me back to reality. Jack's at the stove in a faded T-shirt, beer in one hand, spatula in the other, dish towel slung over his shoulder. I stand watching for a heartbeat, suspended in time, acutely aware of how much has shifted. And how close we came days ago to crossing a line I swore I wouldn't.

Our eyes meet briefly before Jack looks back at the stove with urgency, jaw tightening as he presses the spatula down.

"Hey," he says, then nods toward the back porch. "We heard you'd be hungry. Grill's on. I'm toasting buns."

Dawn leans against the counter and grins. "Awww, you two are seriously making us dinner right now?"

"She said *hot and hungry*," Drew calls from the porch. "It was either burgers or barricade the doors."

Jack's dad is on the back deck too, fiddling with the speaker while Jack's mom uncorks a bottle of wine. It's domestic and homey and so bittersweet.

Fifteen minutes later, the baby's asleep, Allie is back in a fresh outfit, and the cheese is melted. The guys pass around plates stacked with burgers and chips, and we follow them out to the deck.

"I forgot how good these cheeseburgers are," I murmur, licking mustard off my thumb.

"You know how Jack is about the importance of the bun." Allie says. "He'll convince himself he needs to switch up the bread, but he always comes back to Arthur's Bakery buns.

Dawn eyes me over the rim of her glass. "Sounds about right."

I don't take the bait. I try not to dwell on the warmth curling in my stomach as I take another bite of burger that feels like a homecoming. Maybe I'm drunker than I thought. Jack's mom's voice cuts through the chatter at the table.

"Lucy," Janice says, "tell us about your art show coming up in a couple weeks. Jack tells me it's going to be at Graham Vale's home?"

I feel the blush creep into my cheeks as my eyes meet Jack's, and I clear my throat.

"Yes, Helen at the gallery invited me to be a part of it. No one can believe that Mr. Vale has offered to host it."

"The whole island has been talking about it," Dawn adds.

"We wouldn't miss it for the world, Lucy," Janice says.

Jack's dad leans back in one of the cushioned wicker chairs, swirling the wine in his glass. The string lights overhead catch just enough of the silver in his hair to make him look faintly mythic.

"You know," he says, gesturing lazily toward Jack. "I remember when this one used to sneak Lucy in late at night."

Jack groans immediately. "Dad."

"I'm just saying," he continues, ignoring him. "He didn't realize I'd be sitting out back in this very chair reading my book. I'd watch the whole thing happen in slow motion. Lucy tiptoeing over," Jack's dad glances over at me with delight flashing in his eyes, "like you were in a heist movie. Jack holding the gate open like he wasn't the worst lookout in the world."

The whole porch cracks up.

I can feel my heart start to race as I shake my head. "I don't remember that."

"Oh yeah? I doubt that," he grins, lifting his glass in salute. "But you both did a great job pretending not to see me. I respected the effort."

I glance across the porch and meet Jack's gaze. I do remember sneaking over late, after we thought everyone was asleep. We apparently weren't as sneaky as we thought we were. There's warmth in Jack's eyes now. I look away first. Take a sip of my drink.

Dawn stretches her legs across a chair and fans herself with a coaster. "Remind me again why we're not just ending the night right here?"

"*Because*," Allie says, bouncing slightly in her chair, part-built in rhythm from baby duty, part-excitement. "Karaoke needs us."

Jack looks from Dawn to Allie to me. "You're actually still going?"

"So it seems," Dawn breathes out. "And don't act like you're not coming with us."

Drew glances at Jack then shrugs. "Already cleared it with Mom and Dad. Free babysitters."

Jack sighs dramatically. "Fine. But I'm not singing unless Lucy does."

I sit up straighter at the unexpected attention. "What is this, a threat?" I ask, unable to hide my pleasure.

He smirks. "More of a promise."

The soft thump of bass and amateur singing spills from upstairs as we pull up to Daddy D's. A red neon sign greets us, an invitation and a dare, as we climb the wooden staircase two by two, the steps worn from years of nights just like this. At the top of the porch, the music hits full force, Whitney Houston's "I Wanna Dance With Somebody," layered with laughter, cigarette smoke, and the unmistakable crackle of too many voices singing at once. Inside, it's packed. It's not a huge space, but it's pulsing with life. Everyone's on their feet, dancing and singing along.

We barely get three steps in before I spot Sloane and Dinah in the middle of it all. Sloane in something fluttery and unapologetically short, Dinah holding court in a tight tan crocheted mini being spun by a guy who looks a few years younger than us.

"Thank God," Allie yells over the music. "Glad to see our social committee is already here. Is it just me or does this crowd keep getting younger?"

Sloane spots us and waves us over. Drew and Jack head to the bar for drinks. I glance around the crowd nervously but can't help deflate a little as I notice who isn't here. Noah still hasn't texted back. Maybe he's busy. Maybe he's avoiding me. Maybe I'm relieved he's not here.

The front door opens behind me and I turn, but it's just a tourist in cargo shorts. Dinah's saying something about some boy band member from the nineties showing up at karaoke last week, but I can't focus. I'm nodding along in the right places, but part of me is tuned to every shift in the room, every new arrival.

"Ladies and gentlemen," the DJ drawls into the mic. "A very special welcome to a dear friend of the house."

I glance around, curious, until the first unmistakable chords ring out. The crowd reacts a second before I do, cheers erupting, and someone whistles.

My eyes swivel over to Jack, still by the bar, and I can practically hear his groan, amused and resigned. Like someone just reminded him of a bet he made freshman year of college. His ears have already gone pink.

Before he can protest, a couple of regulars gently herd him forward, laughing and clapping him on the back affection-ately. The DJ grins and hands over the mic with a flourish.

"It's tradition," someone behind me says. "He crushed this song years ago, and they refuse to let it die."

He takes the mic, and everyone's already singing the open-ing line of "Stubborn Love" by the Lumineers without him.

The entire bar swells with him, a chorus of off-key voices and glowing faces. A loose circle forms around him, people dancing and bumping shoulders and shouting harmonies. It feels less like a performance and more like a homecoming.

Our eyes meet and I find bashful amusement, maybe a hint of surprise, that this ritual hasn't faded. When he reaches the last line, the crowd is deafening, and I can't fight the smile spreading across my face.

He laughs, ducking his head as he hands the mic back, cheeks flushed. "Okay, okay. That's enough." His gaze sweeps the room until it lands on me. Like muscle memory. It hits me all at once. All those times he sang it like a private message.

Drew hands me a drink as the next song flashes onto the screen, and he points at Sloane and Allie weaving back toward us, two microphones held triumphantly overhead like they've just won a prize.

I squint at the monitor. "No way," I whisper. REO Speedwagon, "Keep On Loving You."

"*DRIVE ME CRAZY!!!*" Sloane screams like we're thirteen again.

I'm pulled straight back to the summers we spent watching that movie on repeat, quoting every line, rewinding the scene where Adrian Grenier and Melissa Joan Hart scream this song at the top of their lungs. The crush we all had on him was basically a teenage girl requirement.

Allie thrusts a mic toward me. "Come on. I know you know every word."

The opening chords hit, and without even looking at each other, we fall into place, Dawn taking the high harmony she definitely can't hit, Sloane choreographing moves we've never practiced, Allie nudging her shoulder into mine like she used to do at sleepovers, and Dinah living out her pop-star fantasy.

Halfway through the first chorus the crowd is singing along. Dinah turns and points at me dramatically, which makes me burst out laughing and lose the line. When the last note fades, we get multiple whistles as we make our way to an available corner, a little sweaty but glowing.

"Adrian Grenier would be proud," Dinah says.

"As would Melissa," I add.

"My legs are trembling," Allie groans, collapsing onto the bench.

"I think half the bar recorded us. It'll be on Daddy D's socials by midnight," I say, cheeks flushed.

The music changes again, some guy doing an energetic and jumpy version of "Mr. Brightside." The air is sticky, my skin's buzzing, and I'm happy to be surrounded by people who know me. I forget to keep checking the door.

That's when Jack slides in next to me.

"So," he says, nudging my shoulder. "You still remember all the words?"

I look at him sideways. "To what?"

He gives me a look.

"Oh no, Jack."

"Oh yes, Lucy."

"We haven't done that in forever," I argue.

"Then I'd argue we're due."

"Jack!"

But he's already up, walking toward the DJ. I groan, but it's pointless.

A few people cheer when Jack's name is eventually called over the mic. Of course they do. He knows most of the people in here from summers spent fixing boats and helping with sailing club. He remembers birthdays and bartenders' names and who just opened a golf cart rental out of their garage.

He turns and gestures to me like this is some kind of encore we'd planned, and suddenly everyone's looking. Dawn's clapping. Dinah's whistling. Allie is already filming.

"You're a menace," I mutter, reluctantly pushing myself to stand as the first twangy guitar strums fill the room.

Jack hands me a mic as I step beside him, grinning. "Don't be shy, June."

I roll my eyes, but when I start singing, the words fall out like they never left. Jack takes his part, that familiar glint in his voice, and by the second verse we're leaning into it, just enough to make it a show.

We move without thinking, the way you can with someone who's been around long enough to know your timing, your tone, your tells. The crowd loves it. People are swaying. Someone yells, "get married already!" I blush.

We hit the final chorus, and Jack grabs my hand as we belt out the words, forgetting the rest of the room.

The last note fades, and the crowd erupts. I turn to him laughing and jump into his arms before we both take an exaggerated bow. There's a twinkle in his eye, and it's a reminder of who Jack is when he stops putting so much pressure on himself. And a reminder of how good it feels to be by his side.

As we begin to walk off the stage, something tugs at my vision. I glance toward the door and see Noah standing inside the entrance.

He's in jeans and a white tee, a little windblown. His expression is unreadable, but his smile doesn't reach his eyes. He clearly just watched me sing a well-practiced love song with my ex, and it's impossible not to wonder if there's still something between us.

Noah's eyes are still locked on me as he walks through the loose crowd around us. I know the exact moment he sees Jack's hand drop from my waist. His smile is polite but tight around the edges. His jaw ticks once before he smooths it out. When he reaches me, his hug is one of those one-armed, sideways things.

"Hey," he says, his voice trying for relaxed but not pulling it off.

"Noah," I say, too bright, too fast.

He gives me a small smile, but his eyes flick to Jack and back again, like he's trying to slot a piece of a puzzle into place.

Jack stays beside me, relaxed, hands in his pockets, offering Noah a warm, genuine, *completely unthreatened* smile. "Hey, man. Good to see you."

Noah returns it but slower. "Yeah. You too."

I struggle to focus while someone sings "Just Like Heaven" by The Cure. Noah looks at me again.

"You two looked like you've done that before." The comment has a slight edge to it, like he's working hard to keep it casual.

I tuck a strand of hair behind my ear. "It's an old favorite of my Gran's."

Jack lets out a soft laugh. "She used to play it on repeat. It was hard not to sing along." Jack grins, easy and warm, and the air around us lightens. Noah shifts his weight, taking this in.

"It was good," he says after an uncomfortable pause. "You sounded great."

Jack nods in thanks, even though the compliment wasn't for him, and somehow that tiny gesture makes him seem even more grounded. "She always does," he says simply, smiling down at me proudly.

He doesn't say it in a flirty or pointed way, but it makes my pulse jump. Noah's jaw ticks again, like he's trying to decide what to do with the moment. Then he steps a little closer.

He studies me for a beat too long. "But I liked your barefoot beach performance better." His fingers tap against his thigh, restless.

I huff a laugh as my face heats up. "Well, not everyone gets the exclusive beach performance," I manage, aiming for light but feeling uncomfortable.

Jacob appears beside Noah, all long limbs and easy energy, holding up his hand to someone behind the bar. "Let's go get a beer. Oh hey, Lucy. Jack."

Jack lifts a hand in greeting.

Noah leans in, the scruff along his jaw brushing my skin. Unnecessarily close. "I'm gonna grab a drink, want anything?"

I lift the drink in my hand. "I'm good."

His fingers trail lightly down my arm as he steps away, and his eyes flick to Jack again as he goes, like he's checking whether the touch landed. For the first time with Noah, my stomach flips, but not in a good way.

No sooner has he stepped away than—"Lucy!" Sloane shrieks from across the bar. "We need backup. Dawn just volunteered us for TLC!"

Jack snorts under his breath. I open my mouth, not even sure what to say, but someone jostles past us, and the moment breaks. Jack lifts his eyebrows, amused. "Guess you're up again."

After another rousing performance, I look toward the bar. Noah's still with Jacob, laughing at something he says, shoulders loose now, the earlier tightness gone like it never happened.

"By the way," Sloane breathes at my side. "Why didn't anyone tell me the songwriter was like, *hot* hot?"

I'm distracted as I reply, "He's not your type."

She arches a brow. "What happened?"

I sigh. "He saw Jack and me singing and got a little… territorial. It's fine."

Sloane makes a face. "Hmmm. Well, he's a grown man. He can shake it off." She looks past me. "And speak of the devil."

Noah bumps my shoulder. "What should I sing up there?"

I give him a look. "You're the songwriter."

"Lucy and Noah," the DJ calls into the mic. "You're up!"

Noah turns slowly, a smile creeping across his face like he *absolutely* planned this.

I stare. "You didn't…"

"I didn't," he confirms. "But I can't say I'm mad about it."

Jacob raises his hand. "I may have mentioned something to the DJ."

The screen blinks to life, and I read the title. That slow, sweeping opening. *No.* "No," I protest. "Absolutely not." Dread starts to fill me as I realize I can't get out of this.

Noah grins, grabbing my hand. "'Time of My Life.' It's fate, Briland."

"We are not doing the lift," I hiss as we're handed mics.

"We're doing the lift."

The crowd starts cheering like it's a championship match, *Dirty Dancing* clearly still a fan favorite. I scan the room, searching for Jack. I spot him in the far corner of the bar, watching the situation unfold. He lifts his chin at me, but I don't miss the hurt in his expression. I try to shake off the gut punch of guilt that hits me.

The music swells. Noah takes a step toward me, hand extended, completely unfazed as his voice deepens to hit the opening line.

We start with exaggerated gestures and fake sincerity. I twirl dramatically, he spins me, we channel every school talent show disaster we've ever witnessed.

When we hit the final chorus and he mouths, "the lift?" I shake my head so fast I almost fall over.

He still takes two steps back like he's thinking about it. I lunge and pull him in by the shirt.

"No lift," I whisper. "You'll kill us both."

The final chorus crashes down and we throw ourselves into it, arms wide. Noah's playing it up now, singing with his hand on his heart, eyes locked on mine like he's in on the greatest joke in the world. It's actually fun. It's on the surface. The exact opposite of my song with Jack.

As we make our way to the porch for some fresh air, Noah catches my hand, lacing our fingers just long enough to make his presence known.

"Admit it," he says, low in my ear. "You had the time of your life."

I roll my eyes. "You're insufferable."

"But memorable," he says.

I don't answer. Because I'm too busy scanning the crowd. Jack's gone. There's a vague swirl of people near where he was standing, but no familiar outline. I don't know what I feel. Relief? Guilt? Disappointment?

Noah's still beside me, flushed from the spotlight, his shoulder brushing mine. Someone offers him a high five. He takes it, laughing, but I just stand there. I'm not sure if I'm dizzy from the club lights, or from the way the night keeps rearranging beneath my feet.

Chapter Seventeen

"SO," DINAH SAYS, "ARE WE STARTING WITH YOUR DUET WITH Jack or your *Dirty Dancing* reenactment with Noah?"

I grimace. "Must we?"

The pink sand packs beneath my toes as Dinah and I walk the length of the beach. I've spent the day painting upstairs, but now that the sky is starting to bruise, it feels good to get some fresh air.

"Oh, come on," she says, nudging me lightly with her elbow. "You and Jack had all of us in a nostalgic spiral. Even my impenetrable heart was feeling it. And then you and Noah went full rom-com."

I sigh and shake my head. "It was fun. I was drunk. It was drunk fun."

"Which part?"

I roll my eyes at her, at myself. "All of it."

She laughs. "And?"

"And confusing?" I admit, slowing my pace. "I don't know what I'm doing. I like Noah. He's arguably a great guy. But then I bump into my ex every other day, and, well you know how it is with him, Dinah. I can never resist Jack. One look from him, and I'm on fire. It's always been that way for me. I'm beginning to think it always will be." I rub my thumb along the strap of my tank, nervous energy buzzing. "No matter how much distance I try to build, the second I see Jack, it's all still there. The history. The way he sees me, it's like no one else can. And I," I swallow, hating how true it is, "I don't know how to un-feel that."

I kick at a shell in the sand, frustration knotting in my chest. "And what makes it worse is I don't even have to *see* Jack for it to start. I'll be out for a run, or making coffee, or folding laundry, and bam. A memory will blindside me. Like the way he used to wrap me up in his oversized hoodie when I was cold, or the way he always makes sure I'm okay at a party. With just a glance, I know he's reading me."

"And not just this summer. It's been happening for the last two years. But being back here, it's like there are little fingerprints of him on everything." I feel my voice thinning as my throat goes tight. I'll go days without seeing him, but I'm still seeing him everywhere."

I drag a hand through my hair, annoyed at myself. "And when he's actually *there*? When he looks at me like he did last night? All of me just boils over. Ugh. I hate this."

"Do you really though?" Dinah asks.

No. I love it. I love being anywhere near Jack. That's what makes this so frustrating. We aren't together anymore. It's been nearly two years. Confusion clouds my head as we pass some teens throwing a lacrosse ball.

"I hate that I don't know how to *not* feel it, if that makes any sense," I wince. "I can promise myself I've moved on, but the second Jack shows up, or the second I even *think* about him showing up, everything tilts. I'll be minding my business, and out of nowhere I'll think, I wonder if he remembered sunscreen on his morning run. Who does that?"

"Someone still in it," Dinah says, squeezing my wrist. "And then there's the hunky musician …"

"Noah surprises me. He's new. But with him I sometimes feel like I'm trying on a version of myself not with Jack, just to see how it fits."

Dinah bumps my shoulder. "Just make sure you're being true to the girl I know and love."

The breeze pushes a strand of hair across my cheek. I swipe it away, annoyed at myself. And how annoying I must be to listen to. Dragging my toes through the sand, I watch the way the pink grains collapse and slowly fill back in.

"Noah's fun. And smart. And so cute. Exactly who I'd fall for if I met him back home."

"Sounds promising."

"But," I start, acutely aware of how much I'm obsessing. "Jack. That spark between us just won't die, no matter how much time passes. *Almost* kissing him was hotter than anyone I've been with the past two years."

"Damn," Dinah exhales. "You've got yourself a solid love triangle, Luce."

I groan and cover my face with my hands. "I just want someone who will choose me, make a life *with* me, and not expect me to squeeze into the sidelines of theirs."

Dinah leans over and hugs me. "And you deserve that. Now, want me to distract you with the latest on *my* tragic love life?"

I glance over. "The French guy?"

Dinah nods. "He left the island this morning."

My eyes widen. "Already?"

"He texted. Something vague and charming about rescheduling dinner in another time zone."

I frown. "Classic rich guy fade. Do you think he'll come back later this summer?"

She shrugs but isn't quite pulling off nonchalant. "I hope so. Which is gross."

"It's not gross," I say. "It's hopeful. There's nothing wrong with that. But you deserve more."

Dinah wraps her arm around my shoulders. "Coming from the girl tangled between two decent and hopeful men, I'll take that as a compliment."

We're halfway back to my house when thunder bellows, low and rolling. I glance over my shoulder, and the sky behind us has gone dark. A storm is barreling our way. "Let's pick up the pace before we get caught in that."

Dinah looks back and pulls out her phone. I watch her lips curl with mischief as she reads. "The group chat says rainy game day at Jack and Allie's."

By the time we climb the back steps, the storm breaks, fast and hard, the way island weather always does. Rain sheets off the roof, pounding loud enough that I can't hear whatever Allie says when she opens the door, Felix propped on her hip.

Inside, the living room is warm and cozy. Drew's at the counter mixing a pitcher of margaritas. For as long as I can remember, we've gathered here on rainy days for cards. The teams change, the jokes evolve, but the ritual never does.

"All right," Allie says from the rug, cross-legged, shuffling the deck in her hands. "What are we playing?"

Another crack of thunder rolls overhead as the front door bangs, and Thomas bursts in, T-shirt soaked. "Euchre or bust," he declares, already sprawling onto his stomach and digging into the bowl of popcorn.

Two minutes later, Sloane and Dawn tumble in on a gust of wind, hair frizzing at their temples. Sloane drops onto the arm of the couch beside me. "Are you dealing Euchre? I still don't understand this game."

"That's apparently the point," Dawn says. "Jack just makes up the rules as he goes."

"I do not," Jack calls from the kitchen. He appears with a small bowl of pistachios. "I enforce the rules. There's a difference."

He grins at me, and I return it with a wave, my neck heating up at the reminder of how I just spent the last twenty minutes pouring out my soul to Dinah. Thank goodness he has no idea.

"All right. Teams." Allie is practical and efficient as she pulls her braid over one shoulder. "Lucy, you're with Sloane. Thomas and Jack are together. Dawn and Dinah, you'll play the winner. I'll ref until Felix takes a nap and then Drew can be my partner."

Cards are dealt. Popcorn gets passed. Rain hammers the roof in a steady percussion, drowning out everything beyond these walls. The room smells of wet hair, salty air, and butter.

"Lucy, play a good card," Sloane whispers as she lays her first card.

Jack leans forward, elbows braced on his knees. "No cheating," he warns, one brow lifted at the two of us.

Dawn cackles. "Oh, please. Lucy's the only one here who doesn't cheat."

I lay down a card.

Jack studies me over the top of his, then smirks as he lays a trump over my ace. "If it helps, I didn't enjoy doing that."

I squint back at him, "Sure you didn't."

The games unfold the way they always do, with Thomas swearing he's been sabotaged and Sloane insisting she almost understands this time. I try my best to stay focused, but Thomas and Jack beat us anyway. Between rounds I duck into the kitchen to refill my drink. When I look up, I see that Jack has followed me in.

He leans one hip against the counter. "Good game."

"You left early," I blurt. "Last night."

Jack's eyebrows lift, surprised. "You noticed?"

"Of course."

He exhales, rubbing the back of his neck. "Look, I," He hesitates, searching for words. "I didn't want to…make things weird."

The admission hits somewhere low in my chest. "You don't make things weird," I answer.

His gaze flicks up to mine, almost hopeful. "Luce…I—"

Before he can finish his thought, Thomas pokes his head through the doorway and grabs the salt.

"Popcorn is bland as hell. We're up," he announces, looking at Jack. "Gotta defend our title."

Jack straightens, the moment snapping like a rubber band. He turns to me, an apologetic smile on his lips.

"Good luck," I say, looking up at him as his eyes pour over my face.

He steps past me to the living room, but as he goes, his hand skims the back of my arm. Light, intimate, and gone in an instant. I stare at the spot he touched. Outside, thunder rolls again. Inside, the air thickens, with rain, with history, with things unsaid.

Later, freshly showered and climbing into bed, my mind swirls around the Jack that exists this summer and the Jack from two years ago. Present Jack feels more settled, more tuned in and relaxed. Past Jack was preoccupied and distracted. The night we broke up was the final straw. It was the night before my art gallery reception in Charleston. My first real solo show.

"You know I wish I could be there," he'd said.

"You could be."

"Luce…I hate myself for it. Not being there for you tomorrow. I know how hard you've worked on this collection. I am *so* proud of you. If I had any choice, any wiggle room to make it happen, I'd be there. But I have to be at this meeting tomorrow."

A last-minute meeting in New York that his boss pulled him into, something "really important," something that couldn't be moved.

"It's always a client meeting. Or an event. This is one of the biggest moments of my life, and you're choosing work."

I could hear Jack's frustration as he replied, "This *is* for us. For our future."

"I don't want a future where you're not by my side. Where I come second."

There was an empty pause then, almost like a flatline, "Luce."

"I think I need some space, Jack."

The show was packed. Dinah flew in with an embarrassing bouquet of ranunculus. My parents came and pretended not to cry. Gran held court proudly by the guestbook. I smiled until my cheeks ached. But I kept glancing toward the door. Even though I knew Jack wasn't coming, I kept hoping he'd surprise me. This show was everything I'd been working toward. And he wasn't there.

So I stood there in a navy dress I picked because he once told me it brought out my eyes, shaking hands with strangers and hugging friends, pretending the empty space beside me didn't matter.

Chapter Eighteen

JACK

WHEN I SAW THE STORM ROLLING IN YESTERDAY, I KNEW IT WAS
the perfect excuse to see her again. Once I confirmed Allie
and Drew were down for game night, I texted the group and
waited like an idiot until Dinah replied that she and Lucy were
"coming in hot off the beach."

This summer has been the one good thing in the longest
two years of my life. Just being near Lucy again. Even that feels
like more than I deserve. I've been keeping myself on the tight-
est leash possible. No showing up at her door with coffee, no
late-night check-ins. I can't tell you how many times I've had to
shove my hands in my pockets to keep from reaching for her.

And the irony isn't lost on me that for a guy trying so hard
to give her space, I somehow keep ending up in her yard with
a toolbox. I've fixed the beach gate, pressure washed Milly's
front porch, unclogged her sink, filled the Jolly with gas, put
air in the tires, weeded the front yard. She doesn't need the

help, but doing something, anything, makes me feel like I still get to show up for Lucy, even from a distance.

When she told me she needed space, I should've dropped everything and flown to Charleston. Screw the meeting, screw the boss. Even in the moment, I knew I was blowing it.

So this summer, I'm doing it right. Or trying to.

And yeah, if I'm honest, this would all be simpler if Noah wasn't in the picture. He seems like a solid guy, the kind I'd watch a game with under any other circumstances. Which somehow makes it worse, because I understand exactly why she likes him.

I know I can't undo the moment I didn't show up for her. I wasn't going to try for a second chance, because I know I don't deserve it. I just wanted to show up for Lucy in small, steady ways. But now that she's back in my life, I'm going to fight for her. I'll spend the rest of my life making sure she never has to doubt me again.

By seven-thirty a.m., I'm on the beach before everyone else, setting up bins and sorting gloves for the annual cleanup. My parents are on babysitting duty, so the reigns fell to me. The sun's already bright, the breeze sharp with salt, and every time I bend down the sand shifts under my feet. It should keep me busy. Distracted. Focused.

It doesn't.

Lucy arrives with Dawn and Sloane, all morning sunshine and bare legs and that faded blue T-shirt that she stole from me years ago. She tucks her hair behind her ears, and somehow that simple movement knocks the wind out of my lungs. It's unfair how effortless she is just standing there.

"All right, where do we put this?" Thomas calls, holding up a tangled chunk of rope.

"The green bin," I say, pointing.

Before I can take even two steps toward Lucy, Allie waves me over to help untangle a net. Then Dawn needs more bags. Then Dinah asks where to dump a broken crate. A volunteer loses a glove. Someone else needs scissors. Another needs zip ties.

Every damn person on this beach needs something from me, except the one person I want to walk toward.

I catch snippets of her laughter drifting down the beach. Soft and real. It hits me straight in the chest.

Finally, after being yanked in twelve directions, I get a clear path. She's fifteen feet away, bent over tying a trash bag, sunlight catching the loose wisps of hair around her face. She looks happy. Light. Untouchable.

Lucy glances over and smiles at me, her face softening as I smile back and take a step toward her. But then she straightens, pauses, and pulls out her phone. Her forehead furrows as she looks at her screen.

She types something fast, thumbs moving with certainty, then stares down at the screen, waiting. My stomach drops.

I force myself to look away and pull out my phone, pretending I have something to do besides fall apart in the middle of a beach cleanup.

Passcode: 1118. Her birthday. I should change it, but I never will.

By the time I look back up, Lucy is walking in the opposite direction with the others, phone still in hand, moving away from me like it's the easiest thing in the world.

Two teenagers step in front of me, looking like they've been dragged here under protest. "Uh, where does this go?" one asks, dangling a wad of fishing line.

I point vaguely toward a bin without really seeing it.

She's walking away. And I'm standing here holding a trash bag like an idiot who already knows how this ends.

But I can't lose her again.

Chapter Nineteen

I SHOULD BE FOCUSING ON MY MASCARA, NOT THE TEXT THREAD I've re-opened for the third time today. But it's still there on my screen, glowing back at me, highlighting my indecision.

Noah: Are you free tonight?

A week ago, this text would have sent a spark right through me. Now, it just makes me tired. Jack's face keeps looping in my head, tugging at everything I thought I'd put away.

Still, standing in the middle of the beach cleanup, my thumbs type back.

Me: There's a party out at The Narrows
Noah: Is that an invitation?
Me: If you want it to be
Noah: I'll pick you up?
Me: That'd be nice

I regretted responding immediately.

Now my room looks like it's been hit by a small storm. There's a pile of dresses on the floor that didn't make the cut, too sweet, too serious, too *not enough*.

What I land on looks simple. Technically. But it's the kind of simple that takes twenty minutes and three outfit changes. The dress is a double layer of semi sheer mesh in a shade of aqua that catches the light like sea glass. It skims under my collarbone, dips low between my shoulder blades, and clings just enough to feel intentional without trying too hard.

Tonight my clothes are my armor, readying me for whatever comes next.

My makeup is bolder than usual, clean lines sharp enough to hold their own against the dress. I've pinned my hair up, leaving my neck and collarbone bare, framed only by my favorite gold hoops. A dusting of shimmer on my shoulders catches the light, because if there was ever a night for a little extra, it's this one.

I smooth my dress one last time, and head for the door just as headlights sweep across the wall. Right on time.

When I open the door, Noah's already stepping onto the porch, hands in his pockets. And when he sees me, he doesn't speak right away. Just looks, clocking every detail like he's filing it away somewhere.

He gives a tiny shake of his head and smiles. "Damn."

I should say something cool back. He offers his hand like we're walking into a ballroom, not the kind of party where someone will definitely end up in the pool.

"Ready?"

I nod, but I don't take his hand. I loop my arm through his instead.

When we pull up to the party, the estate is lit up, lanterns strung between palm trees lighting the path to the main house, the sound of laughter spilling down the front steps. Noah shifts behind me, placing his hand lightly on the small of my back. His palm stays there as we step inside, just enough pressure to say *I'm here* without needing to say anything else.

It's the kind of crowd that makes you stand up straighter without realizing it, old money mixed with young chaos. The band is tucked into the corner of the veranda, playing a cover of "Come On Eileen." Champagne flutes catch light on silver trays.

Someone brushes past us, and Noah leans in slightly, his lips near my ear. "Every guy here's trying not to stare at you."

I self-consciously glance down.

"I'm the one who gets to," he winks, voice gravely. I feel the vibration of his voice in my stomach and laugh nervously.

We snake our way through the party, stopping for quick hellos. People know him now. Dinah pulls him into a joke before I can get to her. Sloane gives him a once over, then mouths *hot* to me behind his back.

I'm not sure what unsettles me more, how easily he can fit in, or how weird that feels. Noah shifts beside me, fingers brushing my lower back again.

"I like your friends," he says quietly, watching Dinah argue with a man twenty years her senior over a tray of oysters.

His fingers travel up my arm, just enough to make me aware of him all over again. He hasn't stopped touching me since we got here, light and constant, like he doesn't even realize he's doing it. I'm no longer sure how it makes me feel.

"I've been in a lot of rooms where everyone was polished and perfect, and you leave not knowing a single real thing about anyone."

"And this feels different?" I ask.

"This island's different," he says. "People don't bother hiding what they want. It can be messy, but it feels real. Not performative."

I tilt my head. "Maybe. To me, the island's about calm. Mornings on the porch, the ocean smoothing everything down. That's the part that feels real. Not the parties."

He studies me, eyes deepening. "The parties are performance for you?"

"Sometimes."

He leans in. "So, tell me, Lucy, who are you performing for tonight?"

My pulse stutters. Because I know exactly who's attention I want.

I laugh lightly, trying to ease the tension of the moment. "You think you can read me now?"

His gaze flickers, just once, toward the other side of the room, where Jack is talking to a woman I don't recognize.

"I pay attention to the people I like," he says quietly. "Even if it's not in my best interest."

Before I can respond, a hand taps Noah's shoulder. It's a slightly older guy in a white terrycloth blazer, holding two drinks and grinning like they've known each other forever. "Noah, hey man, can I steal you for a sec?"

Noah gives me a glance. A silent *okay if I go?*

I nod. "I'll be right here."

He squeezes my arm lightly as he turns to follow, and I stay planted, sipping my wine, trying to work out that last line. *Even if it's not in my best interest.* What does that mean exactly? That I've become a risky distraction? Because of Jack? I exhale and scan the terrace, pretending I'm not looking for anyone in particular.

"Okay, don't panic," Sloane says, moving next to me.

My stomach plummets. "Why would I panic?"

Dinah and Dawn both turn to us.

Sloane tips her chin toward the bar. "There's a mystery woman over there with Jack."

My eyes travel across the room to Jack in a chambray button-down rolled to the elbows. He's laughing, animated, the center of a group of four. I recognize one of them, but my eyes skip past him and land on her.

She's tall. Magnetic. Her hair tumbles over her bare shoulders in shiny, unbothered waves, like she walked straight out of a beauty ad. And she's close. Too close. I watch as she leans in and touches Jack's arm like it's second nature. Jack smiles at her politely. He says something, and the woman leans in further, touching his shoulder.

The wine is suddenly sharp in my mouth. My skin feels too warm, like I'm overdressed, like there's a spotlight directly on me. The image is already burned in my brain, her hand on his arm, the way he leaned in, relaxed.

I glance to my right. Noah's still talking with his friends, back turned now, gesturing with his glass. I force myself to smile at a server offering a tray of mini fried chicken biscuits and take another sip of wine. I'm fine. *It's fine.*

"Good for him. I don't care if he talks to other women," I lie instantly.

Dinah's hand lands warm at my elbow. "Oh please, she's probably a friend of a friend. Work. Logistics. Something boring."

I force a breath. "Seriously. It's fine."

Sloane studies my face for half a second too long, then pivots like a good friend should. "Okay, well just say the word and I'll go be *terribly* friendly."

"Okay," I say, half-laughing. I shouldn't be bothered by this. But all I can think is that I should be the one by Jack's side.

The band cuts into a version of the Chainsmokers' "Closer," and the crowd erupts as the vocals come in, bodies surging toward the lawn.

Noah appears at my side, warm and grinning. "Dance?"

I glance once more toward Jack. This time when I look, Jack catches me. His face is hard to read. Pensive. For a beat, we just…stare. And then he smiles, but it's the smile he reserves only for me, whether he realizes it or not.

"Sure," I breathe. "We can dance."

Noah isn't a showy dancer, just comfortable and loose. He makes it easy to fall into a rhythm. I let myself laugh as the wine buzz carries me through a couple of songs, but my eyes never stop tracking Jack's movements.

Now he's with Thomas near the edge of the veranda, talking animatedly. The mystery woman is nowhere in sight. Undeserved relief pools in my chest.

We turn with the crowd just as the band launches into "Young, Wild & Free." I catch sight of Jack again. He's angled toward Thomas still, nodding along to whatever he's saying, but the woman is now just behind him, close enough to be in the same conversation.

Jack doesn't seem to see her. But I do. Noah catches my hands and spins me under his arm, our movements easy. He smells like clean laundry and salt air. He looks at me, and there's a moment where the noise drops out.

"You okay?" he asks quietly.

"Yeah. I…yeah." My voice is thinner than I want.

"You sure?" His eyes are careful, searching.

I nod. But there's a flicker I can't shake. Dancing like this with Noah makes me feel kind of dirty. I like Noah, but I'm using him to make Jack jealous. In the middle of a party for everyone to see.

He takes my hand and pulls me back into the dance, and I let him. For a while, it's fun again. We move, drink, laugh. Eventually, the crowd starts to thin, becoming a younger party now. Shoes come off, a group of twenty-year-olds eventually jump in the pool, and the music shifts to a more frantic, last-call kind of vibe. I try to stay in it, smiling, sipping what's left of my drink, but my momentum's fading. My feet hurt. I'm tired.

And every time my gaze wanders, it drifts back to where I last saw them. Jack's gone. She's gone.

Noah leans behind me, his hand light at my waist. "Wanna call it?"

I swallow. "Yeah. I'm ready."

The drive back is quiet, comfortable for him, claustrophobic for me. When we pull up to Lazy Daisy, Noah parks but doesn't move to get out. He turns toward me.

"Want me to walk you in?"

For a beat, the easier option is to say yes. To keep pretending I can feel one thing to quiet another. But I can't.

"That's okay," I say softly. "Thanks for the ride, and for coming with me."

He nods once. "I had fun. I'll call you tomorrow."

I hop out of the golf cart, feet hitting the coral stone. "Goodnight, Noah."

"Goodnight, Lucy."

He waits until I'm inside before driving off. When the lock clicks, the house falls achingly quiet. Which means all I can hear is the noise in my head.

Chapter Twenty

"WHY IS IT SO BRIGHT TODAY?" I MOAN, SHIELDING MY EYES.

"As soon as a table with an umbrella opens up, we're moving over," Dawn says, glancing around and fanning herself with her straw hat. It's noon, and we're sitting on the edge of the bay at Queen Conch. I stab the ice in my drink with my straw.

"You're being weird," she says.

"I'm always weird."

"Not like this." She sets her hat down. "Talk."

I focus on my conch salad, pretending to rearrange it in the bowl. "There's nothing to talk about."

Dawn snorts. "Okay, well I guess I hallucinated you last night at The Narrows."

My throat tightens. "Dawn."

"No," she says, leaning in, elbows on the table. "Listen. I love you. But you cannot stand there on the dance floor staring at Jack like you were watching Lazy Daisy burn down and then sit here and act like everything is normal."

I freeze, my fork hovering in midair.

Dawn continues, determined. "I mean, Noah had you on the dance floor. But Jack had your attention. And every single person in that room knew it. Including Noah"

My pulse races. "I wasn't…"

"You were," she says gently. "And you know what else I saw? Jack watching you right back and trying to convince himself not to wade through the crowd."

My breath catches. "He wasn't."

"He was," Dawn says. "It was the kind of look that makes you want to cover your eyes because you're intruding on something private."

Heat creeps into my cheeks. I look down at my lap, avoiding Dawn's eyes.

"And then," Dawn continues, sipping her water and leaning back, "Noah put his hand on your back, and I swear I felt Jack's heart crack from across the lawn."

I wince. "Stop."

"What?" she says. "Someone has to tell the truth. You didn't look torn. You looked…gutted."

I swallow hard. "I'm not trying to hurt anyone."

"I know," she says softly. "But that's exactly what's happening."

"I think I'm still very much in love with Jack."

"I know."

A long, quiet beat hangs between us. Silverware clatters at another table. Someone laughs somewhere behind me.

I push my sunglasses higher on my nose. "The art show is this weekend. What I need to do is just focus on wrapping up my final piece today."

"Oh okay, we're changing the subject. I guess I'll go with it. For now." Dawn sticks her tongue out at me. "Because I *am* dying to see it all come together. And to explore Graham Vale's house, of course."

"Of course," I smile. "I need to have everything over to the gallery tomorrow morning for framing."

"It's going to be great, Luce. I'm so proud of you," Dawn says, reaching over and squeezing my hand.

"Thanks Dawn." I feel good about this collection, maybe the best I've ever felt about my work. It came from somewhere real. It's not just about the island. It's about everything that's unfolded *on* it. Maybe it's Lazy Daisy. Maybe Gran's somehow nudging me gently toward the truth.

LATER THAT NIGHT THE HOUSE IS QUIET EXCEPT FOR THE LOW roll of the waves outside and the soft scrape of my palette knife against canvas. I'm tapping my foot in concentration, wearing an old, oversized linen button-down covered in paint smudges.

This is the last piece. I've struggled with it the most, but it finally unfolded today. Maybe it was lunch with Dawn and being honest about my feelings for Jack. But I finally found the line. The palette is all soft golds and coral pinks, layered with streaks of that moody violet I keep reaching for. There's a heartbeat to it now.

I'm so deep in it I almost don't hear the knock. Three light taps then a pause.

I wipe my hands on a towel and pad down the stairs. When I open the door, Jack is standing there, hair damp from a shower. I can smell his shampoo. He's wearing a soft green T-shirt and holding a small, wrapped bundle in a dish towel.

"Hey," he says, an apology flashing across his face. "Sorry it's late."

I smile, pure happiness soaring through me at his unexpected presence. "Everything okay?"

He lifts his hands slightly. "My mom was cleaning out one of the kitchen cabinets and found this tucked behind the canisters. She thought it must've been your grandmother's. There's a little tag on the bottom that says 'Margaret.'"

He holds it out, and I take it carefully, unwrapping the towel to find a small ceramic sugar jar. Pale pink with a tiny floral handle. I recognize it immediately.

"Wow, I haven't seen this in years," I say quietly. "She used to stick handwritten notes in it. Like fortune cookies, but sassier."

Jack tilts his head with a little laugh. "Sassy how?"

I smile, remembering. "One of them said 'The prettiest shells are often empty inside.'"

He laughs. "That's not always true."

"She had some hot takes." My cheeks heat as I smile down at the jar.

Jack smirks. "And she was rarely wrong."

I look back up at him. It's just us again. No parties. No other people.

"Well…thanks. For bringing it back."

He shrugs, brushing it off. "Happy to."

He doesn't move to leave.

I rest the jar on the entry table. "I was just finishing my last piece for the show."

His eyes light up. "Cutting it close, aren't you?"

"Very," I smirk. "Helen wants everything at the gallery by nine tomorrow morning so she can get them framed in time before hanging them at Graham's."

"Need any help?"

I wave vaguely in the direction of the Jolly. "It should just take a couple trips."

Jack nods. "That's one way to do it."

A beat stretches out, charged, and before I can stop myself, the question slips out.

"So…who was that girl at the party last night?"

Jack's head jerks up, a look of confusion on his face. "Who?"

"The girl with you," I say, aiming for breezy and failing. "Tall. Green dress. Looked like she stepped out of a Bond movie."

He blinks then lets out a breath that sounds almost like disbelief. "Oh. No." He shifts his weight, something softening in his expression. "Thomas knows her somehow. I just met her."

"Right," I say lightly, though my pulse is pounding. "She just didn't look familiar."

Jack studies me and says, very quietly, "Did it bother you?"

My throat tightens instantly. "I just…no. I was just curious."

He doesn't move, doesn't look away. Then, "Because I hated seeing someone else beside you."

The world tilts. I feel it. In my ribs. In my breath. Everywhere. Before I can think better of it, the admission tumbles out of me in a whisper I barely recognize as my own.

"I hated it, too."

Jack inhales sharply. That's all it takes to shift the air between us, suddenly thick, close, and electric. He steps in slightly, not touching me, but near enough that I feel his body heat.

His voice drops. "You're the only one I want beside me, Luce."

It hits me like a wave and suddenly I'm breathless. I want him so much that it feels dangerous. My knees feel unreliable.

My brain is a scrambled mess of *what if* and *not yet* and *oh God, is this real.*

I take a small step back to steady myself.

"Jack…" My voice fails me for a second. I swallow. "That… means a lot. More than I know what to do with right now."

He freezes, brows pulling together.

I shake my head quickly. "You didn't do anything wrong. I just," I exhale shakily. "My head's still a mess with this show. Let me catch up to myself before I say something I'm not ready to say."

Jack nods, slow and understanding. "Okay," he says quietly. "Whenever you're ready."

He gives me the gentlest smile, and it almost has me biting back my words and pulling him into me. But then clears his throat.

"Well." He gestures toward his house. "I should let you finish up."

"Oh," I say, startled by how disappointed I suddenly feel. "Right. Yes. I should…get back to it."

"Good night, Luce," he says.

"Night, Jack," I manage.

Chapter Twenty-One

IT'S POURING. NOT A LIGHT SHOWER BUT A FULL TROPICAL TAN-trum, sideways wind, soaked palms. It's been coming down for the last hour at least.

I pace through the house, hair twisted on top of my head, coffee clutched like a lifeline. The hall is lined with paintings, leaning against walls and door frames. My work, my voice, all of it ready to be transported into town to be framed and hung under lights for strangers to examine and judge.

I look at the time: 8:20. Framing starts at nine. Helen made that extremely clear. And she's already squeezing framing in for me as a favor, so there's no room for error. Which means I need to get moving since it's going to take me a few trips to transport all these paintings.

I step back, heart racing, doing quick math I can't make work. Even if I wait a little longer and I double up trips, there's no way to keep everything dry. And these are canvas. Water is not part of the palette.

"Damn," I mutter, opening the front door and gazing out at the water pouring off the porch roof. My stomach knots. I'm halfway back inside to start gathering towels when I hear the soft crunch of tires.

I stare, and through the sheets of rain make out a large white work van pulling into my drive. The windows are fogged slightly, windshield wipers thudding. It's pouring so hard that I can't see who's sitting behind the wheel until the driver's side door opens and out jumps Jack. He's wearing a rain jacket, hood half off, dark hair dripping at the edges. He lifts a hand like this is all very normal.

"Morning," he calls over the monsoon, stepping onto the porch. "Figured you weren't planning an art baptism today."

I stare at him, stunned. "Whose van is this?"

"Jay's. I called him when I saw the forecast this morning and asked if I could borrow it."

I gape at him, rain dripping from his sleeves, my heart doing something weird and fluttery.

"You didn't think to text me?"

He shrugs. "I figured if I asked, you'd refuse the help."

I open my mouth. Then close it, holding back a grin. "I don't know. I was starting to feel a little desperate."

Jack walks past me and opens the door wider. "Well? Shall we start loading?"

The air leaves my lungs in a shaky rush. "Yes. Please. Let's load her up."

We load quickly, working in rhythm, barely speaking. He handles everything like it's second nature, covering, stacking, securing, shielding. He even brought towels.

By the time we close the van doors, we're both dripping. I run around to the passenger side and climb in, slamming the door behind me as thunder cracks in the distance. The rain drums hard against the roof of the van. I push wet hair off my face, breathing hard, my heart still racing from the chaos, from memories of the last time Jack and I sat next to each other in the middle of a storm. Jack turns the key, and the engine rumbles to life.

"All set?" he asks, glancing over.

I nod. "All set. Thank you, Jack," I say quietly.

He smiles, fiddling with the windshield wipers.

The rain is still pouring when we pull up in front of the gallery. Jack backs the van into the parking spot right in front of the entrance and hops out. He opens the back carefully, stepping in to shield the canvases from the storm as I run ahead and push open the gallery's door.

Helen appears a moment later, her black hair pulled back in a low twist, glasses slipping down her nose. "There you are," she says, clearly relieved. "I was hoping the rain wouldn't throw off the morning."

"Never," I say, sneaking a grin at Jack.

We work quickly. He moves each piece with careful precision, like they're museum grade. No dragging. No tipping. He holds them like they matter. When we reach the last canvas, the one I finished late last night, he pauses after he sets it down.

He doesn't look at me, just keeps staring at the painting. His expression softens. "This one. It feels like you."

I nod, feeling a prickling behind my eyes. "I finished that one last night."

"Okay, thank you dream team," Helen says, reappearing with her measuring tape. "Now let *my* team do our thing. Lucy, I'll see you Saturday night at Graham's. Don't forget to come early so we can get some photos." She pauses, folding her arms in front of her. "I still can't believe it's happening. All summer I've been waiting for the other shoe to drop. But it really does seem to be coming together." She starts to shoo us out the door. "Okay, you two go be cute somewhere else so I can get to work."

I blush, flustered. Jack smirks but doesn't comment. He just wipes his hands on his jacket and heads for the door.

I'm curled on the couch in dry clothes, and the rain still hasn't stopped. The house smells faintly of paint and honeysuckle from the candle I lit an hour ago. The quiet feels like it might split open if I move.

I keep replaying the morning in my head, the moment I opened my front door and Jack was just…there. Like this was the only place he could have possibly been.

The thing that keeps getting me is how he knew exactly what I needed before I even understood how stressed I was. He saw the problem, obviously the Jolly wasn't going to cut it, and literally saved my day.

That's when it hits me, really hits me, that this isn't the Jack who missed my Charleston art show because of a client meeting. This is someone different. Someone whose first instinct now is to show up, not apologize for why he didn't.

And I don't know whether that makes me relieved or terrified. Because if he's changed…then I have to consider the possibility that we didn't fall apart because we weren't right for each other.

We fell apart because he wasn't ready.

And now he might be.

The thought steals my breath all at once. And something inside me is suddenly waking up.

Chapter Twenty-Two

THE NIGHT OF THE SHOW, I ARRIVE AT GRAHAM VALE'S HOME early. Driving Gran's light blue Jolly through the open gate sends a rush of chills down my body. This is really happening. My debut on Harbour Island. A place that has been as important to me as home. It is home.

The drive curves through a long stretch of manicured lawns and palms lit from below, glowing like stage props. The house appears slowly, sprawling and low against the horizon. From the outside it looks almost austere, but the light pouring from its windows lights the whole place up, like it's been eagerly waiting for visitors all these years.

I park and am greeted by Helen leaning out of the back of a supply van, a stack of red dot stickers in her hand. She's wearing a long, silk hammered dress that I recognize from Shine, a cute boutique right around the corner from the gallery.

"Lucy, you are stunning in this white dress," she calls, her voice gleeful. "You're not going to believe this place. Let's get some photos of you with your pieces before the crowd starts to flood in."

I smooth a hand over the dress automatically. It was Gran's. I found it in the back of her closet the first week I moved in. The fabric had yellowed, the seams were tired, but the bones of it were beautiful. Nanette, the island seamstress, worked her magic, and now it feels like something out of a dream. Soft, simple, perfectly fitted, like it always belonged to me instead of hanging forgotten.

Wearing it tonight feels like walking into this moment with Gran at my back. Like the best parts of her, her courage, her warmth, her quiet confidence, are stitched into the lining.

I follow Helen through the wide front doors and into an octagonal-shaped entry that could swallow me whole. Massive blue and white vases bristle with palm fronds and island greenery, and every wall seems to hold a story. Some are Graham's iconic prints, others are clearly pulled from his private art collection, and tonight, the pieces from the show.

"Careful not to trip," Helen says as I slow to take it all in. "This house has that effect. You forget where you're going."

We pass through a long hallway lined with white-painted tole palm fronds, as Helen introduces me to the other featured artists in their spaces. At last we enter a long side room, the kind of place meant for games and lingering parties. Helen stops in the doorway, her eyes glittering.

"I put you in here," she says conspiratorially. "Your paintings against Graham's photography The sunset light pouring in later. It'll be magic."

I step into the room and turn slowly, taking in the spotlit canvases, the way the colors seem to breathe against the backdrop of the room. For a moment I can't speak.

Helen watches me with satisfaction. "The press is going to eat this up. Graham Vale hasn't opened his doors in over two decades. He's practically a ghost. And now? Every national magazine is either here on the island or on standby. His house. His collection. *You.*" She squeezes my arm.

I swallow, the weight of it all settling in. "But why now? Why is he doing this?"

Helen shrugs. "Who can say? Maybe it's the art." She tilts her head, studying one of Graham's photographs featuring Harbour Island's famous Lone Tree, a large driftwood that arrived during Hurricane Andrew in 1992. "Or maybe he's tired of being alone."

Someone calls her name from down the hall and she slips away, leaving me alone, my heart pounding. I'm still turning slowly in the center of the room, my gaze caught between my canvases and Graham's stark black and whites, when I feel someone in the doorway.

"Not too shabby at all," a man's voice says, warm and low.

I turn, startled, to find him there. Graham Vale. Taller than I expected, though stooped now with age. His hair is white, swept back neatly, his linen jacket hanging loose on his frame. But his eyes are bright and mischievous, as if they've seen everything and kept most of it to themselves.

"You must be Lucy."

I nod quickly, setting my phone down before I drop it. "Yes. And you're…"

"Old," he interrupts with a laugh, extending a steady hand. "And apparently hosting parties again. What do you think of that?"

I take his hand, surprised by the strength in it. "I think it's generous. And unexpected."

He smiles, glancing around the room. "Ah, I've spent too many years hiding behind my own work. It's good to be reminded that art belongs to the living, not just to the archives." His gaze drifts back to my paintings. "These sing, you know. Not politely either. They demand."

The words catch in my chest. "Thank you," I manage, though it feels inadequate.

He folds his hands behind his back, strolling a few steps into the room. "I first came to this island nearly seventy years ago. Different world then. Fewer tourists. But even then, the light was the same. It's the most beautiful light in the world. It's why I never quite managed to stay away."

I watch him, trying to imagine this elegant man decades younger, camera slung around his neck, chasing sunlit scenes of parties and beaches. I know from photos that he was handsome, and he still carries it. "You've been coming back ever since?"

"Every chance I had," he says, and something soft flickers in his expression. "The island has a way of keeping pieces of you. Sometimes you don't realize it until you're here again, standing in front of something, or someone, that reminds you of what you left behind."

He looks away, back at my painting closest to him, and the mischief returns to his smile. "Now, forgive an old man. I promised Helen I'd make the rounds before this place fills up. But I'm very glad we finally met, Lucy."

"Me, too," I say quietly, touched in a way I can't quite name.

He gives a small bow of his head before slipping back into the hall, leaving me in the golden light, my heart thrumming.

Helen waves me over to the corner where a woman in all black is adjusting her camera lens.

"Lucy, this is Jasmine, the photographer. She's going to get some shots of you with your work."

The photographer positions me in front of one of my larger canvases. "Just stand naturally. Chin down a bit. Perfect." The shutter clicks in steady rhythm as I shift, smile, laugh when Helen says something ridiculous from off to the side. For a few minutes it feels like I've slipped inside one of Graham's old photographs, posed but not stiff, caught mid-laugh, distilled into nothing but light and angles.

Once the front doors open, the quiet shatters. Guests spill into the house, first in a steady trickle, then in waves. Strangers with glossy hair, tailored clothing, fine jewelry, voices lifting as cocktails appear in hands like magic. A woman with a press badge leans past me to snap photos of the room. Another jots in a small leather notebook, eyes flicking between my paintings and the plaques beneath them.

I spot Dinah first, her emerald green skirt trailing like liquid, already charming someone I don't recognize. Then Sloane sweeps in, sleek in a black one-shouldered dress. She loops her arm through mine with a grin.

"This is incredible, Lucy," she says, eyes sweeping the room. "It's your strongest work yet. I'm amazed by you. I'm going to send photos to a few of my art clients." She squeezes my arm and steps back to take me in. "You're glowing, by the way."

"It's nervous sweat," I correct. "There's a difference."

Helen waves me over to meet a couple visiting from Lyford. I do the rounds. Smile. Shake hands. Thank people I've never met for their kind words. A woman tells me she's drawn to my use of color. Someone else says they want to step inside my beach path painting. It's thrilling. My cheeks heat as another flash goes off.

Allie, looking statuesque and baby free, is grabbing a puff pastry from a passing tray, her parents on either side of her. They wave me over, her mother pulling me into a strong hug, her father squeezing my hand with genuine pride.

"How does it feel, Lucy?" Allie says, her eyes bright. "It's like half the island's here for you."

I laugh, brushing it off, "I think it's more likely everyone is here to see this house."

I gesture around at our beautiful setting, and I notice Jack, standing near one of my canvases, deep in conversation with a well-dressed older man. He holds his glass loosely, leaning in as the man speaks, then gestures toward my painting. The small tilt of his smile is unmistakably pride, dangerous in how directly it makes my heart swell.

When he notices me watching, a flicker of amazement crosses his face, then something warmer. He excuses himself and makes his way over.

"Well," he says, his voice low but teasing, "seems your fan club's multiplying by the minute."

"Including you?"

His grin deepens. "I'm the president of your fan club. Always have been."

The way he says it makes my heart flutter. I nudge him lightly with my shoulder. "Don't let the champagne go to your head."

"Too late," he murmurs, his eyes steady on mine.

He leans in, close enough that I catch the faintest trace of his cologne. "You deserve this night, Luce."

"Literally everyone is here," Dinah interrupts as she materializes next to us with a Rum Dum in hand. "I saw our old surf instructor, Sam. Remember how cute we thought he was?

And the guy who fixed our water fountain last summer is over by the bar. And I'm ninety nine percent sure that woman with the scowl over there by the window is that old lady Heim who used to chase us off Grandfather's Beach."

I follow her gaze, my laugh coming hard at the memory. "Oh my God that *is* her. I could never forget that scowl."

Dinah straightens her skirt, already angling a step in that direction, mischief glinting in her eyes. "Want me to chase her out?"

"Sorry to interrupt," Helen leans in, cheeks flushed with movement. "But I thought you'd want to know, three pieces have already sold."

My heart skips. "Wait, really?"

She nods. "The seascape with the coral sweep. The shadowed stairway. And the one with the fig trees. Two to that man over there," she gestures subtly with the edge of her clipboard.

I follow her line of sight to the man I'd seen Jack talking to earlier.

Dinah turns to look as well. "Collector?"

I glance at Jack, but he just takes a sip of his drink.

Helen nods. "A very esteemed one."

My eyes sting suddenly, which is not what I expected. It's not like this is my first sale, or even my first show. But this collection means something more to me. It came from somewhere deeper. I blink hard, pretending it's just the lighting.

"Hi, Noah," Dinah announces, looking just past me.

I turn just in time for him to sweep me into a hug, lifting me off the floor until my feet dangle.

"Lucy, this is incredible. I'm so proud of you," he says as he sets me down, his gaze sweeping over the walls.

"Thanks," I manage, smiling.

Noah nods a hello at Jack, "Hi Jack."

"Hey man." Jack meets my eyes again before clapping Noah on the back and excusing himself.

"This house feels like the kind of place where if you set down a glass without a coaster, someone appears out of thin air to scold you."

I shake my head, laughing. "I think someone would just come and remove it before you even realized it had been taken."

"I'm glad you came," I continue.

"Wouldn't have missed it." He says and slips his hand over mine for the briefest second. A quiet squeeze. And with all the noise pressing in, I suddenly feel like I can't breathe.

"I'm just going to take a lap," I say, gesturing toward the hallway. "Check out the other rooms."

He nods easily. "Go. I'll be around here."

I slip away to explore the rest of the house, curious to see where the other artists have been installed. Each room is its own world, sculptures under spotlights, watercolors pinned in perfect rows, photographs layered with shadows and light. The chatter changes with each doorway, reshaping from critics to collectors to friends gossiping over cocktails.

I run into Dawn, her mother, and Milly outside the room with the watercolors. We catch up for a few minutes while we discreetly people watch.

I weave down a quieter hallway lined with photographs. My heels click against the polished floor, the buzz of the party softening with each step. The walls in this part of the house are lined with Graham's vintage photographs. Sunlight on tennis courts, women in wide-brimmed hats, men balancing cocktails by the pool. All glamorous.

One photo catches my eye.

A woman by the pool, her back to the camera. She's in a swimsuit, at least the bottom half. Her top is missing, discarded on the chaise behind her, with a silk scarf knotted around her hair. She's turning, at the presumed tail end of a laugh, the curve of her bare shoulders and spine catching the light. It's artistic, yes. Elegant. But intimate in a way that makes my skin prickle.

I step closer, my eyes narrowing. The scarf. The gingham-patterned bottoms. I know them.

I've seen them before, in another photo. A different version of this day. Only in that one the woman's in her full bikini, scarf tied in her hair, smiling at the camera, with a wedge of watermelon balanced in her hand.

The room tilts as the connection hits me. It's Gran. Twenty-something, alive in a different way than I've ever seen. And the man behind the camera didn't just capture a moment. He knew her.

I've never heard Graham's name pass Gran's lips. Not once. In all the stories she told me, all the summers and dinners and long walks, he never existed. And yet here he is, not just present but close enough to capture her like this, close enough to know her body, her ease, the moment just after laughter. My mind scrambles for logic. A coincidence. A model. Someone who looked like her. But I know better. This wasn't a stranger with a camera. This was someone she trusted, someone she let see her with her guard down. The realization makes my pulse thrum in my ears. If Gran had a relationship deep enough to leave this kind of trace and never mentioned it, what else lived quietly in her life.

I steady myself against the wall, the edges of the hallway blurring. This isn't just art on the wall. It's a secret hung in plain sight. Deep breaths. In and out. The music and laughter from the main rooms pulse faintly down the hall, tugging me back.

By the time I rejoin the party, my smile is stitched back in place. I weave toward my room, the air buzzing thicker now with bodies and champagne. The room is lit with a warm pink cast from the sunset over the bay just outside the windows. My canvases glow under the spotlights, guests clustered in front of them, murmuring, sipping. A new pair of journalists huddle by the doorway, one snapping photos of the guests, the other scribbling quick notes.

Helen passes, cheeks flushed with victory. "You're a hit," she mouths, brandishing her clipboard like a scorecard before disappearing again.

I catch sight of Allie and her parents still near the center, the three of them radiant with joy. It steadies me. The hum of conversation dips as Graham Vale enters the room. He doesn't call for silence, but the crowd gives it to him anyway.

"I was told I'd forgotten how to throw a party," Graham says, his smile dry, "so I thought I'd prove otherwise." A ripple of laughter. He lifts his glass, glancing at the walls.

"Tonight we celebrate not only the artistic quality of this island, but the artists who keep its spirit alive. Some of us have been coming here for seventy years," a wince and a chuckle, "and some of us are just beginning to add to its story."

He continues, his voice warm and measured, "Truth is, I've hidden behind my photographs for too long. Tonight belongs to the artists who still have the courage to stand in front of their work. These artists remind us why we return to this island. Their work reflects not only what we see here, the beaches, the gardens, the light, but what we feel here. The people. The belonging. The possibility."

He lifts his glass, his gaze skimming across the crowd before lingering on me. My chest tightens, heat blooming at my collarbone. I raise my own glass, careful not to let it tremble.

Applause breaks out, loud and effusive. A ripple of camera flashes follows as Graham steps aside, swallowed back into the throng. As the crowd exhales back into chatter, I drift toward my friends huddled near the grand piano.

"Can you believe this?" Dawn says. "I almost believed that man was a myth."

Thomas laughs. "Back in the day this was *the* house. Champagne pyramids, models by the pool, and more staff than furniture."

Noah shakes his head. "Feels like stepping into another era."

I smile, nodding when the conversation tilts toward which island party has ever come close to touching Graham's. But my focus keeps drifting, because all I can see, burned behind my eyes, is that photograph in the hallway. The scarf in Gran's hair, the intimacy of the moment. I'd like to go find Graham right now and demand an explanation, but I know it's a conversation best saved for another time.

I sip my champagne and laugh at the right moments, but the sound feels distant in my ears. I glance around, and my eyes land on the striking brunette from the Narrows party, the one I had seen with Jack. She's across the hall, her arms looped easily around the neck of a man so arrestingly handsome it almost hurts to look at him. She kisses him full on the mouth, laughing against his lips.

Relief floods me so suddenly it's ridiculous, even though Jack had already explained. I laugh softly to myself. Silly. I was silly. But I'm lighter now, as though the ground beneath me has settled again.

I turn to head back toward the others when a voice standing a few feet away in front of one of my smaller beach scenes grabs my attention. She tilts her head as she studies the painting for a moment.

"I don't know why I love it. I just do," she says to her friend beside her, her voice low but certain. "And that's the best kind of love."

I stop. The words hit like a soft echo. My grandmother used to say that. Exactly that. About songs, about strangers, about dresses on hangers. She never needed a reason. Just a feeling. The woman lingers a moment longer, then moves on. I stand there, watching the place where she'd been. Where my painting still hangs.

And for a second, I wonder if maybe Gran's still here. Tucked into the brushstrokes. Slipping words into strangers' mouths.

Chapter Twenty-Three

I'M STILL RIDING THE BUZZ OF IT ALL WHEN HELEN TEXTS.

> **Helen:** 9 sold. NINE. I give it a week for the
> last three to go. Maybe less if this buzz
> keeps up.

I stare at the message. Nine. I should text her back something witty or charming.

Instead I type: Thank you. For everything, Helen.

We ended with a nightcap here at Lazy Daisy after a long and very late dinner at The Landing. Dawn, Allie, Dinah, Sloane, and me. A table full of love and rehashing and someone spilling a Ginger Fro, The Landing's infamous cocktail, and insisting it was a blessing.

My Loeffler Randall heels from last night are still abandoned on the jute rug, and a prosecco bottle sits in the kitchen sink like it needed somewhere to hide.

I'm rinsing my coffee mug when I hear a soft scrape outside. I step onto the porch, expecting a delivery, maybe one of the girls circling back for something they left behind.

Instead, it's Jack. He's halfway up a ladder, one foot braced against the roofline, garden shears in hand. A palm frond sways, heavy and green, until he clips it clean and steadies himself against the shingles.

"Are you…pruning my house?"

He glances down, a sliver of a smile. "This one's been dragging across your roof. Bad for the shingles."

I step barefoot into the yard, shielding my eyes against the sun. "I didn't notice."

"You would've," he says, climbing down. "Eventually."

"You could've just told me," I say.

He drops the frond down and dusts his hands against his shorts. "Relax," he says, grinning. "I'm not auditioning for a landscaping gig."

I laugh, shaking my head. "Yeah, but you didn't have to do it."

"It's not a big deal." He shrugs, already reaching for the next branch like climbing onto my roof with garden shears is the same as grabbing the mail.

And that's Jack. Always fixing what no one else notices, brushing it off before anyone can thank him.

WITH THE SHOW OVER, FOR THE FIRST TIME IN WEEKS I DON'T have a deadline pressing down on me. No canvases waiting to be finished. No openings to prepare for. The quiet should feel like relief. Instead, it feels restless.

I'm perched on the barstool in the kitchen and pulling over the basket I've somehow ignored since I got here. A messy tangle of old receipts, pocket change, a Bahamian newspaper clipping, a pack of Coral Sands matches.

I thumb through everything absently. My mind keeps looping back to Graham Vale. To the photograph in his hallway, my grandmother with her scarf and beautiful wavy hair. To the way his gaze lingered on me during that toast. He must have realized who I was. I can't stop wondering what happened between them, what they were to each other. Whether anyone else ever knew.

And I can't stop wondering if it was just a single photograph, a fleeting summer afternoon. Maybe Gran was just modeling. But I don't think that was it. Graham Vale and my grandmother. How had it happened? Did she know my grandfather then? And why had she never breathed a word about it?

My fingers slip past a stack of yellowed receipts and catch on another photograph, tucked deep in the basket. I draw it out carefully.

It isn't posed. Gran is in her sun hat, standing in the front yard, her hands braced on her hips, a smirk tugging at her mouth. And beside her, kneeling at the fence line, dirt streaking his forearms, is Jack. His head is bent as he presses soil down around the base of a bougainvillea, a laugh ghosting across his lips.

My breath snags as I pull back. It looks recent, but when was this taken? His hair is shorter, her smile is familiar and wry. I flip it over. Gran's neat and slanted handwriting trails across the back:

For when it blooms.

I turn it back again, my eyes tracing the fence line, the thin stalks barely reaching the first rung. Newly planted. I know that fall. I remember when the blossoms first began to take at Christmas. My chest tightens. We'd broken up just before this. I didn't know he came back then. Gran never mentioned it.

The weight builds, a stinging behind my eyes. Because suddenly her words return to me, spoken in that offhand way she sometimes did, like tossing breadcrumbs I wasn't ready to follow.

The one for you will plant something he might never get to see bloom. And he'll do it anyway.

I hadn't understood them at the time. It was last summer, and I was curled at the other end of the sofa, knees pulled in, still wearing the dress from dinner. Being here without him made it worse in a way I hadn't expected.

The old house creaked around us, the way it always did when the wind blew in off the water. *Gilmore Girls* murmured in the background, the soft glow of the TV spilling light across Gran's sofa. It was our forever comfort show. Gran said Emily Gilmore was misunderstood. "She makes the show," she'd claim, which I argued was incorrect, because clearly Lorelai made the show.

Gran reached for her glass, swirling the wine, studying me over the rim. "You'll not like this," she continued, "but sometimes love needs a little space to figure out what it wants to be."

I tried to laugh, but it caught in my throat. "What if it figures out it doesn't want to be anything at all?"

Out the window, the ocean breeze swayed the tops of the bougainvillea beginning to grow along the fence, rich magenta petals stirring lightly. Gran's gaze lingered there a moment before she spoke again.

She smiled, soft and simple. "Then maybe it isn't. Or, maybe it wasn't meant to grow just yet."

That moment had stayed with me, stubborn as roots. And now, staring down at Jack in the dirt, Gran smirking beside him, it feels unbearably, impossibly true.

Without thinking, I tuck the photo into my back pocket and walk the path up to Milly's cottage.

"Hey Milly." I hug her after she lets me inside, holding the photo out to her. "Do you remember this?"

She looks down at the photo, then smiles like she's back in that moment.

"Oh, sure. You remember how your grandmother used to go on about how she wished she'd planted something colorful by the fence?" Milly rinses a dish, remembering. "Well, what do you know, Jack shows up one day with gloves and bougainvillea. Didn't even knock. Just got to work."

I blink. "She didn't ask him?"

"No, honey," she chuckles. "That boy didn't need asking."

Milly dries her hands and looks at me. I burst into tears.

Chapter Twenty-Four

MY SANDALS SCUFF AGAINST THE SHELL-LINED PATH AS MY MIND runs over what I'm going to say. The photograph is still imprinted in my mind. My grandmother, laughing, glowing, her bare shoulders caught in the light. The kind of photograph that's captured a stolen moment.

I knock. For a minute, I think he won't answer. Then the door swings open and Graham stands in the middle of the doorframe.

"Lucy," he says, surprised. "Did you forget something?"

I hold his gaze. "I saw the photo of my grandmother."

Silence hangs between us. He steps back, a quiet invitation. "Why don't you come in."

I follow Graham into the room where my art hung. He gestures for me to have a seat on the sofa and disappears. Time suspends as I wait. When he reappears, he has a stack of photos in his hand.

"She was younger than you must picture her," he begins, passing me the first photograph. "Not anyone's grandmother. Not anyone's wife. Just Margaret. Restless, radiant, impossible to ignore."

I turn the photo in my hands. She's caught mid-laugh, holding a giant pineapple on top of her head at a Bahamian fruit stand. My throat tightens.

"I met her the summer before she met your grandfather," Graham continues. "She was on the island helping a cousin with their children. I was shooting by day, running wild by night. We collided…and the world tipped over."

The next photo is more candid. She's sitting in a beach chair reading *Pride and Prejudice*, knotted hair damp from the sea, Graham's shadow stretched long across the sand. Another is more daring: a bathing suit strap sliding down her shoulder, her smile aimed straight at the camera. Not posed. Intimate in a way that makes me blush to see her like this, not as my grandmother, but as a beautiful young woman.

"But we were young," Graham says softly. "And when she left that summer, she never came back to me. By the time I saw her again, she was wearing your grandfather's ring."

Another photo, her head tipped back in sunlight, eyes closed, ocean spray frozen in the air. She looks so alive I almost expect to hear her laugh.

His gaze drifts to the stack of photos. "These weren't meant for the world. They were hers and mine. Proof of who we were before life asked us to be anything else."

He places the last photo in my hands. She's midair, jumping off a dock into the turquoise water, laughing over her shoulder toward the camera.

"But didn't you see each other again?" I ask. "This island, it's so small. You must have crossed paths."

"Oh sure, plenty. We were friendly, your grandmother, your grandfather, and me. I had great respect for him, your grandfather. And she was obviously madly in love with him."

Graham studies me for a long moment, then he gestures toward the photographs. "With me, she burned. We were saltwater and fire, but fire can't sustain itself forever. With your grandfather, she found steadiness."

I swallow hard, because I know what he's saying isn't only about the past. The words cut deep, an inheritance as clear as the photographs. For the first time, I see Margaret not only as my grandmother, but as a woman with her own loves, her own choices.

I leave Graham's with more than answers. I leave with artifacts, and a clearer lens on my own heart.

The sun casts long shadows that stretch across the pink sand as Noah and I walk. We're both quiet, the kind of silence that once felt electric. Now it feels like waiting.

I clear my throat. "I've been trying to find the right words."

Noah doesn't press, just patiently watches the tide.

"I care about you," I say finally. "And I'm grateful for this summer, for you. You made it lighter than I thought it could be, when I wasn't sure how to face this island without my grandmother. But," I exhale, "I can't keep pretending I don't know who my heart belongs to."

His nod is slow and steady.

I swallow. "I didn't think it was true. I wanted to see if this could be something real."

"It was," he says, keeping his eyes trained on the shoreline. "But sometimes we're not the whole song. Sometimes we're just the bridge."

I nudge him with my elbow, a smile tugging despite the ache. "You weren't just the in-between, Noah."

"I know," he says. "You were good for me, too, Lucy."

The tide inches higher, foam wetting our toes.

"I want you to find everything you're looking for," I tell him. "Not just with the album. With your life."

A smile pulls at his mouth. "We'll see about everything. As for the album…" He hesitates, then finally looks at me. "You, this island, pulled something out of me this summer. The kind of thing I didn't even realize I was holding back."

I feel the ripple of his words, the flattery, the ache. To have been good for him. To have been part of his music. But I know what I need isn't just to be someone's spark. I want to be the place someone stays. The place they return to.

I step closer, wrapping my arms around him. He exhales, folding me in. His arms tighten once then loosen just as quickly. When we step back, the sky has gone the pale, iridescent color of the inside of a shell.

By the time I get home, Dawn, Dinah, and Sloane are waiting for me on the back porch, claiming chairs and cushions like it's their living room.

Dawn pops open a fan she found somewhere in my house. "Well? What have you gathered us for? You look like you have big news."

I laugh, tucking my legs beneath me. "Depends on your definition of big. I broke things off with Noah."

Dinah's eyes widen, dramatic as always. "Just like that. You don't bury the lede, Luce."

Sloane leans back, unsurprised. "How'd he take it?"

"Pretty well. I knew I couldn't give him more than this summer, and it didn't feel fair to drag it out."

Sloane nods. "Better to end it before it turned messy."

"Definitely trying to avoid messy," I murmur.

Dawn crosses her legs, gaze narrowing just enough to make me squirm. "So…does Jack know?"

The question hangs there as I shake my head, pulling my hair into my elastic. "Not yet. And even when he does know… what will it mean? If Jack and I try again…and it falls apart again, I don't know if I'll be able to put myself back together."

The porch goes quiet for a breath, cicadas buzzing in the dark.

Dawn leans forward. "Lucy, we all know you are it for Jack. And he's spent all summer showing you that he's changed. That he's ready."

Dinah sits up, eyes glittering. "I think it's time you find out if this is it. And you never have to worry about putting yourself back together. You have us for that."

It hits me all at once, how rare it is to have people who pull you forward instead of holding you back. How lucky I am that mine see me clearer than I sometimes see myself. It steadies me in a way nothing else can. My heart stops skittering long enough for the truth to land. I want this. I want *him*. And I'm finally brave enough to say it, at least to myself.

I know what I need to do.

Chapter Twenty-Five

I WAKE UP BEFORE MY ALARM. IT'S ALREADY WARM, AND I KNOW the courts will be brutal by mid-morning. Still, I'm weirdly energized, like my body knows something is coming.

This isn't your average pickleball game. It's a Harbour Island fundraiser, which means custom paddles, pristine tennis whites, courtside charcuterie, at least one friendship hanging in the balance, and a lot of money raised.

And Jack will be there. I haven't seen him since he was pruning my roofline, not since I found the photo of him and Gran. Since the weight of it anchored itself.

By the time I pull up to Romora, the courts are already full. The faint thump of music drifts from a speaker some teens tucked into a palm tree. Players are milling around in matching sets and visors, casually hitting balls back and forth, like no one's been secretly training for this all summer.

I tuck my visor over my ponytail, sling my Lazy Daisy tote over one shoulder, and head toward the courts, scanning the crowd. I find Jack right away, dressed in a perfectly fitted white polo and shorts. He's standing near the fence line talking to someone.

"Damn," Dawn says as I walk over. "If we're going down, at least the pictures will look good."

I grin, spinning in my white pleated skirt. "You think we'll make it past the first round?"

"Depends on who we're up against," she laughs.

"When are we up?" I say.

"Two matches from now. Wanna grab a bite and warm up?"

I tug my visor lower as we move toward the clubhouse porch, where the refreshment table looks like it was curated by a wellness content creator with a Pinterest addiction. There are sliced fruit skewers—pineapple, papaya, kiwi, topped with edible flowers that look almost too pretty to eat. Mini croissants are stacked next to a dish of guava butter. Energy balls dusted in shredded coconut line a rattan tray, and there's a row of pressed green juices sweating quietly in glass bottles beside a Frosé machine already running in the corner.

The tree speaker is playing Gracie Abrams now, and I grab a juice, not because I'm thirsty, but just to feel like I'm doing something. Something to focus on besides Jack stretching, arms overhead, shirt lifting just enough to show a flash of taut, tanned skin. He turns, catches me looking, wipes the sweat off his brow with the hem of his shirt, and winks.

"Oh, he caught you," Dawn murmurs, popping an energy ball in her mouth and offering me one.

I take a bite even as my pulse thumps in my throat.

Dinah and Sloane join us, assessing the table. "Y'all, it's nine-thirty in the morning and people are already playing like there's a trophy involved."

"There is," Sloane says, gesturing toward a nearby table. "The Rooster Cup."

I follow her gaze. Sure enough, a gleaming ceramic rooster stands tall between a stack of towels and a branded cooler. Bright red comb, puffed chest, and a gold pickleball paddle clutched delicately in its beak.

I'm delighted. "Well now we *have* to win."

Dawn nudges me again. "Agreed. Let's go warm up."

We step onto the court to rally, and Jack walks past us toward the sidelines, dragging his paddle along the net like a dare.

"Morning Luce. Dawn," he says, catching my eye.

I roll my shoulders back, trying to look composed. "Morning Jack."

His gaze drops quickly to my mouth and then back up. "You look nervous."

"I'm not nervous," I insist, tightening my grip on my paddle.

His voice softens, low enough that only I can hear it over the chatter of the sidelines. "You bite your lip when you're nervous."

I didn't even realize I was doing it.

I let out a tiny scoff, more air than sound. "…stop trying to distract me, Jack."

The girls cheer from the sidelines like we're in high school again. I toss the ball in the air, hit a serve toward Dawn, and tell myself I didn't try harder because he's watching. By the time our match starts, the crowd has thickened. An oversized whiteboard with the brackets is set up on an easel, manned by a stern-looking gentleman in tennis whites. A drone whirs overhead. I hit three surprisingly decent shots in a row, and Jack claps softly from the sidelines and mouths something to me that I can't quite make out.

Dawn jogs back into position, waving at me. "Earth to Lucy."

I shake my head, trying to collect myself. "Right. Yes. Game face."

But my game face has left the building. When we rotate sides I nearly trip over my own sneakers walking to the baseline. I send my serve straight into the net.

"It's okay, shake it off," Dawn says.

"Totally," I say and then return the next ball straight into the net. Again.

On the next rally I manage to connect, but the shot sails high, a perfect lob for the other team to smash back at us. Dawn lunges, saving it at the last second, then shoots me a look over her shoulder.

"You're trying to kill me," she says, laughing.

I bend forward, laughing. "Luckily you're fast."

I try to focus. Slow my breaths. It doesn't help. I whiff another return, then yell something that earns a look from the older couple playing next to us.

"Okay, what's happening?" Dawn asks. "You're playing like someone who just got emotionally flash fried."

"I'm fine," I insist, determination setting in.

From the sidelines, Jack's leaning against the fence, still watching. Even if I hadn't looked, I would have known because I can feel his eyes boring into me. I exhale, hard. Grip the paddle tighter. And this time, when the ball comes my way, I'm ready. I return it clean and fast, right past the girl waiting at the net.

Dawn lets out a little whoop. "There she is."

I flash her a look. "Just needed a minute."

Next serve, I hit a sharp backhand, surprising even myself. Someone in the small crowd claps.

I steal a glance at Jack, talking to Allie and Drew.

"Nine—seven, one," I say, tossing the ball in the air and sending it across the net with a satisfying thwack.

We win our match, not by much, but enough to earn high fives and a cold towel from the tournament staff, which feels like victory in this August heat. There's a break before our next match, so I grab a fruit skewer and head toward the porch to watch Jack as he steps onto court three.

He's paired with Thomas, and they're both irritatingly good at pickleball. Their opponents are a couple from London who have been coming to the island for a few years now, friendly but clearly out for blood. Jack catches me watching as he reties his laces, and I straighten and turn away.

Dawn flops down next to me, out of breath. "I couldn't catch your eye to save me. I just got cornered by Barefoot Jimmy going on and on about the fish he caught this week."

Barefoot Jimmy is a true island character, perpetually barefoot, with a weathered face and an endless rotation of fishing stories that somehow all last at least ten minutes.

"Let me guess," I say. "Biggest one he's ever seen."

Dawn groans. "He said the fish had better footwork than half the players out here."

I laugh, patting Dawn's hand sympathetically, as we both turn our attention back to the courts. Jack is playing now, and he's beautiful to watch. Understated in that infuriating way where he's clearly in control but it looks like he's not even trying. I've played with him before; I know his game. But he's more strategic now. Whatever edges he had have only gotten sharper.

At one point, he wipes sweat from his forehead with the back of his wrist and sends me a heated look.

"Jesus," Dawn murmurs next to me. "Even I'm turned on."

I turn so fast my ponytail brushes my cheek and find her smirking at me. I give her a friendly shove, laughing.

On the next point, Jack fakes a drop shot then slams the ball down the midline. Thomas claps him on the back as he moves into serving position. I take a long sip of my water. I can feel the heat crawling up the back of my neck.

Dawn and I applaud after Jack and Thomas win their match. "Well, well, look who decided to show up today."

Thomas grins. "You're welcome for the entertainment."

Jack laughs and refills his water bottle before sinking down next to me.

"Impressive," I say, blocking the sun with my hand as I look at him. "It almost looks like you've been practicing."

He shrugs, unscrewing the cap. "Good partner."

Thomas claps his hands on his knees. "Finally. Some appreciation."

Dawn tosses Thomas a towel. "You're covered in sunblock and smugness."

"Better than sunburn and regret," Thomas quips, wiping the sweat from his face and sliding his sunglasses back on.

We talk match stats and court gossip, but Jack stays mostly quiet, eyes on the court.

And then, softly, just for me, "Scoot over, you're hogging the shade."

"You've got an entire side of this step," I laugh, sliding an inch.

Jack leans in, close enough that I feel his breath on my ear. "Yeah, but your side looks better."

Dawn pats my knee. "C'mon, Luce, we're up again."

I stand, giving Jack a look I hope comes off cooler than I feel. "Don't miss me too much."

His grin deepens. "Impossible."

Our next match is tighter. Dawn and I hold our own, though. There are long rallies, some honestly impressive saves, and a moment where I hit a sharp angle shot that gets applause from the sidelines. My pulse kicks up. When I look over, Jack mouths something behind his water bottle.

I squint.

He mouths it again, slower this time.

"That. Was. Hot."

I turn back to the court, cheeks flushed, but not from the heat.

A few points later, I misjudge a bounce and miss it completely, and from the sidelines, I hear Thomas yell, "She's only human!"

We lose by two points, close enough to taste, which somehow softens the blow. Handshakes, paddle taps, a few sweaty congratulations. By lunch time, a polished Palm Beach couple lifts the Rooster Cup, cameras flashing.

My friends scatter with plans to meet on the beach in thirty. Back home, I rinse off the salt and sunscreen, slip into my most flattering red bikini, and twist my damp hair into a braid.

When I walk down to the beach, the group is already forming, towels scattered under a couple of umbrellas. Someone's dragged a few beach chairs out, but most people are sitting in little clusters or lying back on elbows.

Dinah's hunched over someone's speaker, connecting her phone to queue up her playlist. "No offense, but if I hear 'Uptown Funk' one more time."

Jack's standing near an open cooler. He's changed into navy swim trunks and is nodding at something the person next to him said, but a second later, he looks up and finds me through the crowd with a smile.

I head to where Dawn and Sloane have claimed a patch of sand under one of the umbrellas. I take a sip of the grapefruit seltzer I'm handed, cold, fizzy, and just sweet enough to feel celebratory.

Dawn clinks her drink against mine. "We played well today."

"And we all looked great doing it," Sloane says, stretching her legs out in front of her. "Which, let's be honest, is the whole point."

I settle back, shaking my head at her, trying to look relaxed. Trying *to* relax.

A shadow stretches across the sand as Jack drops down beside Thomas, just a few feet away. Thomas nods toward our group.

"So, rumor on the sidelines is that the couple you were playing in the last match broke up last week. If that's true, they've got better chemistry on the court than half the married people I know."

"Explains why they were hitting so hard," Dawn says.

Allie bends forward, rubbing sunscreen on the tops of her feet. "Who won the tournament?"

"Jasper and Drea, a couple from Palm Beach," Thomas says, shaking his head. "Total upset."

Allie chokes on her drink. "You're kidding. Drea with the arm brace?"

"Apparently it was for show," he says. "Girl's got a killer serve and yells 'yes!' after every single point like she's Serena Williams."

"I heard they hired a coach this year," he adds.

"Of course they did," I mutter as I reach into the bag of sour cream and onion chips that's making the rounds.

"I still can't believe summer's already winding down," Sloane says, fanning herself with the back of her hand. "It flew by faster than usual."

"It always does," Dawn says. "But this one was especially good."

Thomas pops a chip in his mouth. "That's because no one got engaged this year."

"Or broke up mid-season," Jack adds, glancing meaningfully at Sloane.

She throws a chip at him. "That was one time and it was hardly a breakup."

"You locked him out of his rental," Dawn says.

"Because he stole my good beach towel and refused to admit it. What a psychopath."

"And what about the crab Olympics?" Thomas says.

"Which year?" Sloane asks.

"The one where Jack named his crab 'Jeff' and gave it a full motivational speech before the final."

"Hey," Jack says, lifting a hand. "Jeff was a champion."

"He lost in the first round."

"None of that will ever compare to the infamous Man Island camping night," Sloane says, propping herself up on one elbow.

A collective groan rolls through the group.

"That was pure hell," Dinah chimes in.

"We were ill-prepared," I laugh.

"But thank goodness you brought throw pillows," Jack teases me.

"For ambience," I laugh, remembering how I really wanted the setting to reflect a photo I'd saved on Pinterest.

"But then the rain came," Thomas says.

"That's putting it lightly. It poured," Sloane corrects. "Like, biblical levels."

"We had one tarp," Jack says. "Which Thomas tied to a palm tree using shoelaces."

"Hey, it worked for a while," Thomas insists.

"It collapsed on us in the middle of the night and soaked everything," I remind him.

"You slept in my lap the rest of the night," Jack adds, looking at me.

"Because my sleeping bag was wet, and I was freezing," I say in defense, trying not to smile.

"You were humming," he says.

"I was shivering."

"You were humming," he repeats, grinning now. "The Beach Boys. 'Wouldn't It Be Nice.'"

I can't help it, a traitorous smile tugs at my mouth, small and private, like we're the only two who remember it right.

Sloane wipes her eyes. "And didn't someone…yes, it was Dawn, wake up screaming because a stick was in her tent?"

"I thought it was a snake!" Dawn protests.

We're all laughing now. The kind that makes your face hurt and your drink slosh a little.

"I haven't thought about that night in forever," Sloane says, wiping her eyes.

"We should do it again," Thomas says, serious. "Camp on Man Island. One last hurrah before everyone disappears for fall."

Dawn snorts. "Only if we bring real gear this time."

"And more than one tarp," Sloane says.

"And someone other than Thomas ties it down," I add.

"My knots weren't that bad," he mutters.

Jack doesn't add anything. He's just looking out at the water, beer balanced loosely between his hands and a smile still lingering at the edge of his mouth. He glances at me. Just a flick of a look. But I feel it. And I know he's remembering, too.

The conversation drifts around me, and the sun presses hotter against my shoulders. I shift, suddenly restless, the sand gritty against the backs of my legs.

I stand, brushing myself off. "I think I'm going for a swim," I announce.

Jack looks up. "I'll come with you."

I catch Dawn and Sloane share a glance. No one else moves.

Thomas raises his can. "If you skinny dip, I'm taking your clothes."

"We'll take our chances," Jack says, already on his feet.

The water is warm, and I dip under first, working my way past the breaking waves, resurfacing with my hair slicked back and the sun behind Jack's head.

For a minute, we just swim, not away from each other but not quite toward, either. A slow drift as we wait to see who breaks the silence first. The quiet stretches, the only sounds the small slap of water and my pulse in my ears.

Jack treads beside me. There's a pause before he says, "So, no Noah today?"

I glance at him. "No Noah."

He nods once. "How's that going?"

I take a deep breath. "It's not anymore." I keep my tone easy. Like I haven't quietly rehearsed saying it out loud to him. I watch his face for a flicker of a tell, but Jack's hard to read when he wants to be.

"You okay?"

"Yeah. It was the right thing. I'm trying to…" I float for a second, letting the saltwater hold me up. "Make decisions that are best for me. Not just for the summer."

Jack's eyes dart across my face. "He didn't seem like your type."

I raise an eyebrow. "Oh? And what exactly *is* my type?"

He shrugs, that slow, irresistible grin tugging at his mouth. "Someone who likes The Beach Boys at four a.m."

I splash water at him, but I'm smiling again.

Jack tips his head toward the beach. "They're probably placing bets on whether we're gonna make out."

My lips twitch, betraying me before I can stop them. "We *could* really mess with them."

"Could we?" his eyes flash.

I don't answer. I just swim ahead. But when I glance back, he's still watching me, smiling.

BY THE TIME I MAKE IT HOME, THE SKY'S GONE FULL VELVET. I shower again, washing away the salt that's still clinging to my skin.

I'm searching for something to eat when my phone lights up on the counter.

Jack: Admit it. You aimed every serve at me.

Warmth floods my chest, and he's right, I did aim for him during our beach volleyball game tonight.

Me: You were the tallest target

Jack: You cheered any time I missed
Me: I was on the other team. But I did like watching you dive for me.
Jack: I'll dive for you any time
Jack: Rematch in the morning? One on one?
Me: Tempting. But I've got a morning walk with your sister. She's promised me caffeine and unsolicited life advice.
Jack: Sounds about right

And then the three dots pop up again.

Jack: Can I see you soon?

I bite my lip, trying to steady the little jolt low in my stomach.

Me: I'd like that

The dots again.

Jack: I'm not going anywhere

Chapter Twenty-Six

ALLIE'S GOT FELIX STRAPPED TO HER CHEST IN A SOFT CARRIER, her iced latte from Cocoa balanced in one hand as we walk along the water on Bay Street.

"So, Drew's in New York?" I ask, brushing a stray hair off my forehead.

She nods. "Yeah. He had to fly back early for work stuff. It'll be fine though. My parents are here, obviously. And Jack."

I glance over. "Jack's had time to help out?"

She shrugs, adjusting the strap across her shoulder. "He's staying in the guest house, but he's been over at the house a lot. He shows up with breakfast smoothies, hangs with Felix, changes diapers, distracts mom when she's being intense. Honestly, he's been kind of a lifesaver this summer."

I let her words sink in. "It's funny, picturing Jack changing diapers."

Allie laughs. "I know. But he's been great."

It makes me smile, imagining Jack with a baby. That thought should probably scare me, but it doesn't. We keep walking, the breeze coming off the water just strong enough to make the heat tolerable. Felix shifts against Allie's chest, a tiny fist pressed against her shirt like he's making a point.

"He's been sleeping so much better this week," she says, glancing down. "Last week I thought I'd never feel human again, but suddenly he's back to giving me these six-hour stretches. It's like he knew his dad left and decided to give me a break."

I tuck a curl of hair behind his ear. "He's a gentleman."

"He's plotting something," she says, sipping her iced coffee. "He looks innocent, but I know that face."

"That's Jack's baby face, by the way," she adds.

"Oh no."

"Exactly."

We walk into The Sugarmill boutique to check out a trunk show they're having with an Australian designer. Allie finds a dress she loves and says she'll come back to try it on when she has her hands free later. Back out on Bay Street a few golf carts pass. The occasional rooster calls out like he's running late. Allie shifts her coffee to the other hand.

"Jack's stayed on the island longer than I thought he would. He keeps saying he'll rebook his flight and then doesn't." She pauses, then exhales softly. "He's different this summer," she says. "Calmer. Like he's finally letting himself slow down."

Something inside me pulls like the tides. I stare at a cracked seashell half buried in the sand of the road, willing it to anchor me.

Allie sings to Felix, her light and steady voice smoothing over the air between us. But I feel the space she's leaving for me in that silence.

BY THE TIME I FINALLY LEAVE THE HOUSE AGAIN, THE SUN IS setting and I've been pacing for the last hour. Maybe more. I made tea and forgot to drink it. Sliced a mango that had gone too soft on the counter and ate it standing over the sink like it might settle me. It didn't. I stood barefoot in the grass for ten minutes before deciding.

I don't want to waste any more of this summer just thinking about Jack. After circling each other all summer with so many things unsaid.

I look at the bougainvillea in a new way as I step outside the front gate. The ocean's loud tonight, all rolling rush and pull. And the breeze moves through the palm fronds in that whispery way, mimicking how I feel. Restless.

When I reach his guest house, the porch light is on. Smoothing my hands down the sides of my dress, I lift my hand to knock, but before I do, I hear a voice from off to the side.

"Looking for Jack?"

Turning, I see Jack's dad settled into one of the Adirondack chairs underneath the large yellow bloomed Cassia tree, a paperback resting on his stomach.

"Oh hi," I say, trying to keep my voice steady. "Yeah, I am. Is he here?"

He shakes his head and shifts in his seat slightly. "He went down to the beach about twenty minutes ago. Said he needed to clear his head."

My heart stumbles. "Thanks," I say, already backing down the steps.

The path from my yard to the beach is hushed in twilight, the sky gone coral, the sand cool against my feet. I slow as I reach the edge, pausing before the final step.

Pacing just fifteen yards out, Jack's head is bent like he's deep in thought or trying to outrun one. His hands are jammed in his pockets and his shoulders are tight.

Something in my chest loosens. Because he's here. Pacing outside of my house. Like he wants to come up the path but can't. I think about all of the almosts.

The soft claps from the sidelines. The long looks across crowded rooms. Karaoke night. The bougainvillea along the fence. The garage roof. The excuses to stop by. The rain and the painstaking way he helped transport my paintings. The way he quietly showed up all summer. "Everybody keeps Lucy."

Like he's been choosing me in a hundred ways, expecting nothing in return. The errands he never had to run but did. The quiet presence when storms came in, when I lost myself in all the noise of the island. Noah had been the opposite, all fireworks and spotlights, singing his heart on a stage, making sure I couldn't miss him. And I didn't. I saw him. But I was so caught up in the chaos of parties and people and outfits and distractions, willing myself not to notice the person who simply showed up, again and again.

Through the chaos, there was always him.

And now here he is. Pacing this stretch of beach. Maybe we're both trying to find our way to the same place.

"Are you planning to come up?"

His head lifts. He turns. And for a beat, he just looks at me like he's not sure I'm real. Like maybe he conjured me. Then he exhales, slow and uneven, like the air's been caught in his chest all day.

"Luce," he says, like it's a full sentence.

I start toward him, my heartbeat so loud it drowns out the ocean.

His mouth quirks. "I've been thinking about it."

"Thinking hard, apparently," I add, nodding toward the zigzag of pink sandy footprints trailing behind him.

His mouth tips into something sheepish. "Yeah, well. I didn't know if I should show up uninvited."

"You've been showing up all summer," I laugh. "Just never with anything to say."

"I had this plan," he admits. "I was going to win you back this summer."

His eyes flick to mine.

"Then I'd see you, and the plan would just…evaporate. Or get derailed. Every single time. So I just…kept trying again."

Heat climbs the back of my throat.

He swallows. "I kept telling myself to be patient. To wait for you to figure out whatever you needed to figure out. But every night I'd walk this path and wonder what would happen if I just climbed up."

He glances up at the house. "And then," he continues, voice thinning, "one night I opened my laptop to look at flights back to New York…and ended up looking at flights to Charleston instead." He huffs out a laugh that isn't really a laugh. "Old, historic houses with tiny closets and sweeping porches I can't stop picturing you painting on."

My breath catches.

"I haven't gone back to New York," he finishes. "Because home doesn't exist without you in it."

"Luce," his voice drops. "I never stopped loving you. Not once. Not for a minute. Not even when it was easier to pretend I had."

The world goes very still.

"I tried," he says, barely above the tide. "God, I tried. I worked. I traveled. I worked some more. But every time I'd picture the life I wanted…" He shakes his head. "You were in it. Laughing or painting, or just…being. And it stopped making sense to build anything that didn't have space for you."

He takes one small step, then another. Close enough that I can see the fear in his eyes, the hope right behind it.

"If you'll let me," he says, voice steadying, "I'll move to Charleston. I'll mend fences and change your lightbulbs and bring you coffee and plant things I might never see bloom. And I'll never stop trying to win you back." He swallows. "Because love is supposed to feel like this. Present. Steady. Like something you recognize when you finally stop running."

His eyes find mine, tired, terrified, sure.

"I'm here," he whispers. "Tell me if I should stay."

"It was never about a place. Before, Jack. It was about knowing you'd meet me somewhere. That you were willing to show up. Be all in."

He looks at me with years of regret in his eyes. He looks down for a second, then back at me.

"I am all in, Luce," he says. "If you'll let me."

I suck in a breath, the air suddenly too full of everything we haven't said.

"That's all I ever wanted," I whisper.

Jack's voice is low, certain. "There hasn't been a summer, a day, a moment when it wasn't you."

The world stills at his words. The waves hush at the shoreline and the breeze barely stirs. His eyes hold mine, steady and unflinching.

My throat tightens. "Jack…" It's all I can manage, his name carrying a hundred tangled summers.

He takes a step closer, the sand shifting beneath his feet, and his hand reaches out, brushing against mine. "I love you, Luce. I've always loved you, and I *will* always love you."

The breeze dances slowly in my hair, warm and insistent. Something inside me clicks into place, quiet and certain, like it's been waiting for this moment all along. I don't think. I just move. My hands twist into his shirt, and then his arms are around me, pulling me against him, and it feels like finally exhaling after holding my breath all summer. Longer than that.

His mouth finds mine, and there's no question in his kiss. Like we've both known this was coming and the only mistake was how long it took to get here. His arms tighten around me, holding me steady and close. My hands flatten against his chest, working their way up to his shoulders.

When we break apart, I'm laughing and crying at once, salt on my lips that has nothing to do with the sea. He rests his forehead against mine, smiling that slow, infuriating smile.

"About time," he whispers.

I press closer. His hands slide into my hair. The kiss deepens. Sharpens. We've been so careful for so long, but there's nothing careful about this. It's all heat and hunger and *finally*.

He pulls back just enough to breathe. "You taste like mango," he says, slightly breathless.

I laugh, pushing forward again.

"I love you, Lucy," he says, lips brushing mine.

I kiss him again, harder this time, and he groans low in his throat, like it's too much and not enough. His hands slide down my sides, slow and sure.

We break apart again, only barely. "I love you, Jack."

My fingers slip into his hair and he presses closer, like he can't be close enough. A low sound rumbles in his throat, and heat shoots through me in an arc I feel deep in my body.

We break apart only long enough to stumble toward the house, tripping, laughing, hands tangled like muscle memory. Jack bumps the door shut with his heel and I'm pressed against it before I can think, his palm spanning my hip, his mouth finding mine again, not a hint of hesitation left.

"Upstairs," I breathe into his kiss. It's not a request.

We barely make it, pinging off the wall, kissing in broken bursts up the staircase. His firm hand skims the small of my back each time I wobble, steadying me as we hurry, and the familiarity of that undoes me more than the heat. He rediscovers me, jaw, shoulder, collarbone, as if he's cataloguing what he's missed. I'm nearly dizzy with the rush of being wanted this much.

By the time we reach my room, my dress is off and his shirt is somewhere on the stairs. I hook my fingers in his belt loops and guide him toward the bed. He lowers me onto the mattress with a kind of reverence that makes my pulse stumble. The urgency dissolves into something slower, deeper, something that feels like long summer evenings and years of almosts snapping into place.

It feels like returning. Like forever.

It feels like blooming.

Chapter Twenty-Seven

LAZY DAISY IS BUZZING. LAUGHTER SPILLS FROM THE OPEN French doors. Bougainvillea sways in the breeze, framing the porch in a riot of pink. The scent of grilled fish and lime hangs in the air as Jack flips grouper over the flame, a dish towel tossed over his shoulder like he's been doing this his whole life.

He kind of has, I think, watching him from the kitchen window as I top off a pitcher of rum punch. Or at least, the version of his life that leads back here. To me. To us.

"Your man is really committing to the grill aesthetic," Dawn says, sliding up beside me with a stack of mismatched woven placemats. "Is he wearing a linen apron?"

"It's mine," I wink, carrying the pitcher out to the back patio.

The long table is lit by candles flickering in old glass hurricanes, with platters of sliced mango, grilled corn, Allie's orzo salad, and tortillas for the fish tacos. Thomas, Dinah, Allie, and Drew are barefoot on the grass, playing a game of bocce.

Sloane's taking candid videos of the table and narrating them like she's shooting a travel diary.

"Hey, Luce," Jack calls, raising his tongs. "Can I steal you for a grill consultation?"

I cross the patio, weaving through a tangle of coolers. "Do you really need a second opinion, or are you just flirting with your sous chef?"

He grins. "Both," he whispers as he leans down and kisses me.

I lean in, brushing my hand along his waist as I peek at the grill. "Perfect char."

"I aim to please." He drops his voice next to my ear, sending a shiver down my spine.

Dinah interrupts with a shouted request for Jack's playlist. He hands over his phone, and I wander back to the table, pulse fluttering. The golden hour casts everything in that dreamy, pinky peach light that makes even the bug spray bottles look romantic. Jack returns with a fresh platter, dropping a kiss on the tip of my nose before setting it down.

After the plates are cleared and the sky fades all dark and sparkly, Jack pulls me to my feet just as Billie Holiday croons from the speakers. We sway barefoot on the lawn, slow and close, the grass cool beneath our toes.

"You're humming," he says into my hair, barely loud enough to hear.

I smile against his chest. "I always do when I'm happy."

The moment stretches, quiet and perfect, until Sloane's voice cuts across the yard.

"Group photo! Before anyone leaves or sobs!" she shouts, already propping her phone against a pitcher.

Everyone groans but scrambles together. Thomas throws Sloane up on his shoulders, her laugh echoing as she strikes pageant poses. Dinah grabs a candle from the table and holds it above her head like the Statue of Liberty in a silk slip dress. Dawn slides beside me at the last second, slinging an arm around my shoulders.

Someone trips over a cooler. Someone else starts singing off key. We're golden with rum and sun and the kind of friendship that's been earned over decades, leaning in like we always have, like we always will.

Jack slips his arms around my waist just before the shutter clicks, where he's always belonged.

Epilogue

NEXT SUMMER

The string lights sway between the palms, and Jack's cursing under his breath as he wrestles with another knot. His back gleams in the morning sun, shoulders browned and damp with sweat, and I can't stop smiling into my coffee. He doesn't look like the kind of man who plans ambiance, but here he is, hanging lights because I said I wanted the yard to glow.

"Are you sure I'm cut out for this gig?" he calls without looking back, yanking a line taut.

I take a slow sip. "Depends on how straight that last strand is."

He turns, pretending to be offended, hand on his heart. "I'll have you know I'm doing this out of my love for you."

"Funny," I say, smiling into my mug. "I thought you were doing it because you forgot to book a lighting rental."

He laughs, deep and easy, the sound that still undoes me. He steps back to admire his handiwork, then glances over at me. That look. The one that makes everything go still for a second.

"Hard to believe it's been a year," I say softly.

He nods. "The best one."

The breeze lifts the hem of my pajamas. Somewhere down the road, a golf cart buzzes past, faint laughter trailing behind it. The island is stretching awake. Everything feels slow and golden and quietly right.

We're having brunch with his parents in an hour. Low key, just eggs and fruit and an excuse to sit under the big umbrellas on their porch. Jack claims they're relaxed about the whole weekend, but I saw his mom's itinerary printout. There were sub, sub bullets.

We'll walk over soon, past the white gate, now swallowed by bougainvillea. Jack says we should cut it back, but I like it like that—strong, stubborn, and impossible to ignore. Just like the man I love.

My parents arrive tomorrow, and they're staying at the Bahama House Inn with the rest of the early guests. We offered them a room here at the house, of course. They insisted we should have space. I think my mom really just wants an on-call bartender and daily housekeeping.

Milly's thriving. Lazy Daisy is booked solid when we're not here, and she's become the unofficial queen of local rental management. Last month she had to politely evict a couple who tried to shoot a reality dating show in the living room. She says she's going to write a memoir and title it *Bring Your Own Butler*. I told her I'd paint the cover.

The whole thing still feels a little unreal. That we live together in Charleston now. In a little white house on a charming downtown street with green shutters, walking distance to my gallery. On Sundays, Jack strolls to the corner bakery and brings back coffee and croissants, always remembering to grab the paper I like and a weird pastry he wants me to try. We sit together with bedhead and mismatched mugs. It's nothing, and it's everything.

I hold out a hand, wiggling my fingers at him. He crosses the porch in three long steps and leans down to kiss me.

"I like it here," he murmurs.

"You say that every time."

"Doesn't make it less true."

I rest my cheek against his chest. This house. This porch. This person. It's more than I ever wanted. Inside, music from Gran's old radio floats out through the open windows, mixing with the breeze. One song blending into the next, until a voice cuts in.

"Up next, currently number two on the Billboard Hot 100, here's Jacob Alistair with 'Tide Song.'"

The guitar slides in, soft and stripped back. My mug freezes halfway to my lips. The lyrics unfurl, tender and aching, but it's not a love song. And it's not bitter. It's goodbye.

I could've stayed in the tide with you
But I watched the sky instead
Said I'd call in the morning

But I wrote you a song instead
You painted the silence in color
I gave you a half-finished line
You looked for something steady
I was chasing the rhyme

Some people change your rhythm
But not your path
And I think you were the song
Not the aftermath

Jack squeezes my hand, his body leaning into mine.

"Can't blame Noah," he says softly, his eyes on the horizon. "If I'd lost you, I'd have written a whole damn album."

The laugh catches in my throat, breaking the tightness apart. I reach for him, and he leans in without hesitation.

"So," he says. "Still want to marry me?"

I glance at the crooked lights overhead, at the sea glass shadows flickering across his face.

"Yeah," I whisper. "I do."

In a few days, we'll stand on this porch and say it in front of everyone. But right now, it already feels like forever.

WITH GRATITUDE

This book is a love letter to Harbour Island. I want to begin by thanking the island itself, and the beautiful people who call it home, for offering my family a welcoming and inspiring place to belong. It takes only a moment to witness the magic of Briland, and I am honored to be even a small part of its story. You truly are *"Home of the Friendly People"*.

I know without a doubt that *Pink Sand Summer* would not be what it is today without the support, encouragement, and expertise of three incredible women. Abby Abell, Virginia Beard, and Courtney Sakre, your guidance and belief in me have been the gift of a lifetime.

Over the past sixteen months, I immersed myself in the publishing world, listening to podcasts and reading countless articles and interviews. One thing was clear: I could expect the editing stage to be the hardest. Plot twist, Abby, you managed to make it my favorite part of the entire process. You caught plot holes I missed and guided me to tell Lucy's story in a more succinct and enchanting way. You did all of this without a single tear or tantrum on my part, which I had been led to believe were inevitable. Thank you for your many hours and multiple rounds of edits. You helped shape *Pink Sand Summer* into a story that I feel truly confident in, and that is invaluable.

Thank you for championing this book, Courtney. For believing in me before you ever even read a single page. Our paths have crossed for nearly twenty years, and I will never take for granted that you opened a door in this experience and made sure I had exactly the right people by my side. You changed everything.

Thank you for holding my hand through it all, Virginia. For being the very first person to beta read a very messy draft and helping me shape it into a more cohesive story. From that first read all the way through formatting, production, and cover design, you were there for every step, and every question I had along the way. You got into the publishing weeds with me and never once made me feel like any question was too small. I am so grateful you are in my corner.

There's a whole other tribe of women in my life who are my creative inspirations, my advice and hype givers, my confidantes. So much emphasis gets put on romantic love, but female friendships are a different kind of magic entirely. You know who you are.

Thank you, Monique Aimee, for the beautiful cover design. You captured the vibe perfectly. Thank you, Danna Steele, for your formatting brilliance. You're a true expert. Thank you to my incredibly talented audio narrators, Erin Mallon and Jason Clarke. You brought *Pink Sand Summer* to life in a way I never could have, and you were kind and generous with your time and knowledge throughout the entire process. And thank you to my PR team, Jackie Thomson, Annika Moffett, and Cat Hunt, for bolstering this book and being its loudest, most enthusiastic cheerleaders.

On December 31st, 2024, I told my husband, Josh, and our two kids, Lilly and Fletcher, that over the next year I would write a romance novel. You three supported, encouraged, and believed in me every step of the way, and I am unfathomably grateful to have your love in my life. You three are more than I ever hoped for.

And finally, thank you, dear reader. Of all the books you could have chosen, you chose this one, and that means the world to me.

To the BookTok and Bookstagram creators who took the time to share this book with your communities, I see you and I thank you. I know how much time, creativity, and genuine passion goes into what you do. The bookish community is one I am immensely proud to be a part of.

I hope *Pink Sand Summer* transported you to Harbour Island, if only for a little while. If Lucy's story left you with a craving for Arthur's Bakery and pink sand under your feet, then I did my job. And if you're looking for the perfect book club trip destination, I may know just the place. I cannot wait to share more pink sand stories with you. See you there!

Come find me on Instagram at @chassity.evans
or over at @coralhouseharbourisland. I'd love to connect!

ABOUT THE AUTHOR

Chassity Evans is a longtime lifestyle creative known for her warm, detail-rich storytelling and her joyful approach to life. A lifelong romance reader, she loves a perfectly satisfying happily ever after.

After years of sharing books, travel, and the beauty of everyday life with readers, Chassity now brings that same eye for atmosphere and emotional texture to her fiction.

She splits her time between Charleston, South Carolina, and Harbour Island in The Bahamas with her husband and two kids. She loves lattes, singing in the car, and long Friday lunches with girlfriends.

Pink Sand Summer is her debut novel. Connect with Chassity on Instagram @chassity.evans